HAWTHORN HEDGE COUNTRY

HAWTHORN HEDGE
COUNTRY

by

FRED ARCHER

HODDER AND STOUGHTON
LONDON SYDNEY AUCKLAND TORONTO

To my good friend
DON WILLIAMS

CONTENTS

ILLUSTRATIONS

Acknowledgements

†Drawings by William Henry Pyne (1769—1843) in the Mary Evans Picture Library.

*Also from the Mary Evans Picture Library

FOREWORD

FRED ARCHER has written two previous books about village life, in what could be regarded as near the centre of England. The Cotswolds, Tewkesbury, and Bredon Hill have attracted several authors of genius – indeed Stratford-on-Avon is not far away. Fred Archer is in good company, but I find him unique in the detailed truth of his descriptions of country doings, sayings and thought.

His village "Ayshon" is Ashton in the Evesham Vale, remote from main roads, and with the adjacent branch railway now axed. Like Bredon and Beckford it is over-shadowed by Bredon Hill, which is not quite 1,000 ft. high, and yet completely and strangely dominates the wide plain where the Avon joins the Severn.

In *Hawthorn Hedge Country* Fred Archer has written about country life between 1768 and 1813. His characters are fictitious, but as real as Thomas Hardy's *Tess of the D'Urbervilles*. Any countryman over the age of sixty years will have met types such as his squires, his hunting parsons, his tenant farmers and the labourers who know the realities of semi-starvation.

This is not a history book so the young need not be deterred. Dialect is used sparingly, and does not make reading difficult. Technical farming terms are explained in a casual way which does not interfere with the story. This is important for any age of reader in town or country, and yet I did not realise until half-way through the book that Fred Archer was right in explaining terms to *me*. It was not a case of not knowing a word, but that the same term can be used for different jobs in different regions.

He referred to putting single forkfuls of hay in little mounds
before loading to waggons. This I call "pooking", but he said
"piking", which in the North of England means a mound of a
good waggon load, left in the field for many weeks. The author's
art lies in explaining what *he* meant by "piking" before I had
time to misunderstand.

It is largely this skill in casual clarity which makes me sure that
all ages and conditions can appreciate the book. For those who
worked in the years before 1914 it is pleasant to be reminded of
the horse days. Personally I had forgotten that when the carter
rode a huge horse home in the evening he always sat side-saddle.
There was very little deep change in English farming between.
1769 and 1914. We had mowers for grass, and self-binders for
cutting and tying sheaves of grain. Yet in 1912 it was easy on my
father's farm to raise a team of eight men with scythes to mow an
odd six hundred acres of badly twisted corn. Today there is no
man at home who has ever touched a scythe, and I doubt if there
is a self-binder left in the village.

Fred Archer gives a moving but fair account of the Enclosures,
which were still a sore point in my grandfather's youth, and
which have left traces to this day in my own village in the shape
of a collection of tiny fields called "poor lots". In this permissive
age he offers nothing in the way of pornography, but animal and
human breeding are mentioned sanely and frankly. Personally I
had heard of "wet nurses" in my young days, but had not the
slightest idea how things were arranged.

There is so much of the book which I know to be true in every
detail that I accept the author's story where I am ignorant. For
instance, I had a great, great aunt who kept a stage coach Inn,
which my grandfather has described to me. This allows me to
accept that sickles were used for wheat and oats, when I had
imagined that scythes cut all grass and grain. There was a flail on

the barn wall at home, not long ago, but not hinged with eel skin.

This book is genuine, and a real break from the ordinary country literature of today.

RALPH WIGHTMAN

AUTHOR'S PREFACE

Hawthorn Hedge Country is much more a book on the traditions and way of life of Ayshon than a history. The story begins in 1768 and my intention is to depict life as it was lived before and after the Enclosures under Bredon Hill. Sundial Farm exists today, its name having changed many times. The land is the same but now part of a much larger estate. Stories of love, hate, charity and greed are as old as Bredon Hill. The book is a record of life when class distinctions could not be broken or even bent. The good and the bad permeated high and low rural society.

It is so true that as the land varied from stiff clay to limestone, so the speech of the people differed in accent from village to village.

Although living conditions of the workers were poor, farming took a giant step forward during George III's reign. Down the ages people have suffered through sudden changes in a traditional way of life as they did at the time of the Enclosures. I do hope this book gives you a good idea of how life was lived here two hundred years ago.

Ashton-under-Hill FRED ARCHER
April 1970

CHAPTER ONE
Arrival at Ayshon

Michaelmas Day 1768

WHEN GEORGE HEDGECOCK'S waggons and carts brought his live and dead stock on Michaelmas Day 1768 to the eighty-five acre holding known as Sundial Farm, midway up the village lane at Ayshon (Ashton), George found life there following much the same pattern as it had since the sixteenth century. True, some enclosures had been made by Lord Waterford, squire of the neighbouring parish of Beckford and owner of part of Ayshon, and Lady Sarah Fitzwilliam had enclosed Sundial Farm, but the land was still being worked mainly on a four course rotation—wheat one year, barley, then pulse, followed by a year of fallow to rest, clean and aerate the soil.

George was a typical yeoman farmer of forty-five, his wife Anne some five years younger. There were twin daughters, Catherine and Mathilda, seventeen that very day, and a son Mark who was fifteen. George rode his heavyweight hunter long stirruped, cavalry fashion, at the rear of the caravan of working horses, sucking colts, bullocks, milking cows and vehicles just finishing the trail of twenty miles odd from the Cotswold Edge. Harry Steel the stockman and Lijah Hicks, George's waggoner, would be working full-time on the farm and were to live in the black and white wattle and daub cottages opposite the sundial on George's stone-arched gateway.

While Anne and her two daughters walked up the little orchard of cider apple and perry pear trees, the glint of the late afternoon made pretty pictures of golden leaves, green and red apples and bronze pears. The September frost had started to loosen the leaves and a few were already scattered, but the carpet of them was still to come and cover the green turf. Hedgecock, his son and his two men backed the waggons and carts into the cart shed, ungeared the horses and watered them at the stone trough, Lijah working the pump with the rhythm of a blacksmith blowing his bellows. The bullocks, glad to rest after their journey, were bedded down in the yard as Harry Steel carried boltings of straw from the nearby rick. Young Mark fed the horses in their strange stable; he spoke comfortingly to them when they showed him the whites of their eyes, sniffing and snorting at strange fodder in a strange manger. The few milking cows George had brought with him were unwilling to be tied up with chain and chog in the long thatched shed, open at the front and carried by squared oak posts standing on short stone pillars. Milking was finished by the light of two horn lanterns giving enough light to show one end of the cow from the other.

Sundial Farm was a substantial Jacobean house with thick stone walls, mullioned and barred windows, wide elm floor boards in the bedrooms, a spacious cellar and flagstoned hall and kitchen. George Hedgecock had brought just enough furniture for the present and this was roughly arranged by the light of the tallow candles.

The cottages opposite were empty and bare which meant that Harry and Lijah slept that night in the farmhouse after Mrs Hedgecock and the girls had cooked the evening meal, one and all sitting round the kitchen table by the light of the candles and the wood fire. George sat close to the fire next to Anne wondering to himself whether he could afford to pay the £75 a year rent for the farm. Cotswold lands are only a few shillings' rent an acre, he thought, but this will grow twice the crops and make twice the butter. "They do tell me," he said to Anne, "the hams down by Carrants Brook will grow grass waist-high and we have grazing rights down there. Then there's Bredon Hill; some says if you can get a lamb to walk up there in the Autumn, he will thrive and fatten into a useful teg by May. We'll have a good flock on that common land up there.''

Harry and Lijah were thinking of their wives and families left on the Cotswolds.

''Can us fetch our few sticks a furniture and our families with the two 'osses Diamond and Flower tomorrow, Master?'' Lijah plucked up courage to ask George Hedgecock.

''As soon as ever you have milked and fed the other animals,'' George replied, half thinking of his men and half of fat tegs, buckets of milk, quarters of wheat and barley.

''Thank ya, gaffer, we ull be off at fust light, won't us, Lijah?'' Harry said as he got up from the table. ''And now for a shake-down.''

The girls had put ready the oat-chaff-filled bed tick, and with goodnights all round the Cotswold men and women went off to spend their first night under Bredon Hill overlooking Asum's (Evesham's) Vale.

Very early next morning, Lijah and Harry groped with their horn lanterns around the unfamiliar buildings of Sundial Farm. They milked the few cows and noticed how the yield had dropped. This would be only temporary until the cows had got used to the strange surroundings. Harry carried the wooden pails two at a time on his yokes, which seemed to fit his broad shoulders as if they were a part of him. He left the milk in the dairy on the oaken bench near the slatted window ready for Mrs Hedgecock and the girls to deal with when they had breakfasted.

''Not a bad day, Lijah,'' he muttered, as early morning workers mutter. Following the glimmer of his lantern he came out into the inky black yard.

''I a knowed it's only Michaelmas,'' Lijah replied, ''but I beunt a-taking no chances with the weather. I be gwain to gear

Diamond and Flower and when thee 'ast finished fussing round them feow cows, I be ready to start.''

George Hedgecock had already trammed the hogshead barrel of last year's cider, so Harry filled the two half gallon costrel barrels, corked and pegged them ready to hang on Diamond's hames with their frail baskets, each with its ration of bread and cheese, and as a special favour for the journey Mrs Hedgecock had given each of the men a thick chunk of fat reasty bacon.

Although Lijah and Harry were men in their late thirties, the outdoor life, the keen Cotswold wind had given them a rugged appearance. Their faces were as if hewn like the stone walls of their country. Harry was thin, angular, dark and swarthy, his hair and whiskers slightly tinged with grey. His wideawake hat just revealed bushy eyebrows over his dark brown eyes and his long thin nose was constantly in need of wiping; it dripped either because of the cold or because of running sweat. He could have stood six feet tall but preferred to stoop to about five foot nine. He had the nautical roll of a man who had followed oxen, cows and sheep from a lad of seven years old. Lijah had a round, rosy face, wrinkled like a russet apple after Christmas. A kick from a two-year-old colt he was breaking in when he was in his teens had left its mark—a seam of paler pink above his upper lip and a gap where two front upper teeth had been. In men with rounded features, it is quite usual for a rotund body, ample belly and stocky limbs to complete the make up. Sometimes the bottom three buttons of Lijah's waistcoat wouldn't fasten but this morning he had breakfasted lightly—"had a dew bit" as he said—so only two of his waistcoat buttons remained undone.

The road or track from Sundial Farm buildings was steep and rough, joining the village street almost at a right angle. Lijah was carter. He knew his horses, he knew that the mare, Flower, would hold the waggon back as the two horse team made their first descent into the village. Harry led Diamond on the front, a trace horse still carrying the polished brasses he had on the day before, but usually displayed only on market day. "Keep his yud up!" shouted Lijah as he held tight on Flower's mullen so that the bit pressed hard above her tongue and firm against her mouth. Harry steadied Diamond and took him in a wide semi-circle on to the grass verge on the opposite side of the road, his right hand and Diamond's foretop brushing against the ripe blackberry hedge. "Now bring him round. Gently up cup, Flower! . . ." and the right hand turn was perfectly made without the front waggon wheels even scraping against the waggon bed.

For the first two miles, the two men led their horses, down Ayshon's village lane, down Gipsy's Lane to Beckford, then the first rays of the sun peeped over the Cotswold Edge and showed the vale between the hills in its autumn glory. Horse-chestnuts fell from roadside trees, bouncing in and out of the waggon. The odd one fell on Diamond or Flower and prompted them into a short trot.

"How about riding, you?" Harry suggested to Lijah. "You knows what they says in the Army—that's the Cavalry—you gets as much money for riding as ya do for fightin'." Harry tied the rope by G.O. reins on to the ring next the bit on Flower's mullen (or bridge), and with one foot put safely on the hub of the near-side front wheel, he mounted the front of the waggon. "No sore ass for me astride Diamond," were Lijah's words of wisdom and experience, so with the toe of his left boot pushed as far as the instep on top of Diamond's left trace just in front of the back band, he sprang on the back of the gelding. "Whoa, 'ull ya," he spoke softly to him this time as he wriggled himself into a side-saddle position with both heels of his boots pressing against Diamond's ribs and the left trace tightening under his insteps.

With one hand on the mullen rein and the other holding the hames, the horses started again the clip clop along the limestone road not yet churned up by the Winter's rains. Only men born close to the stable could ride so relaxed, so carefree, sidesaddle on a heavy cart horse. Guiding the foremost horse was so simple as to be almost unnecessary, the waggon stayed in the age-old wheel ruts and the horses stayed in the age-old track.

"Just like singing abed," said Lijah.

"Thee wait till the morrow afore thee starts to crow," Harry broke in. "We shan't be at this caper every day, thur's a ell of a lot of ploughing for thee to do at Sundial and the gaffer unt a gwain to keep me just to look ater them feow old cows, he's a gwain to Tewkesbury a Wednesday to buy some fresh calved uns. Oh no, we beunt in for a picnic at Ayshon."

At the foot of Stanway Hill, Harry's shout of 'whoa' to the horses resounded through the woods at the very foot of the Cotswolds, almost where his 'view halloo' sounded when he sighted a hunted fox being chivvied from covert to covert by Lord Coventry's pack of hounds.

Lijah, lounging on Diamond, had been lulled off to sleep "as nigh as damn it is to swearing," Harry told him. "Thee can't expect Diamond to carry thy bulk besides dragging this waggon up Stanway Hill." As the waggon halted for a few minutes, Lijah and Harry viewed what they could of the Cotswold Edge. The outcrops of limestone rock shelved out in the wood as if forming a staddle to one huge rick, the beeches, the oaks and larches lined the narrow track, arching over it cathedral-like, the Autumn sun peeping through the gaps framing windows not of stained glass but of copper, green, yellow and red leaves. The distant purple of the Malvern range stood in contrast as Harry and Lijah had just time for a whiff of bacca in their clay pipes before starting the winding ascent through the woods.

Harry had been wise in bringing the light Cotswold waggon for two horses to pull empty up the hill. "Gee head, Lijah, with Diamond and unrein him so that he can get down to it when we reaches the steepish part." Harry walked by the side of Flower carrying on his shoulder a wooden wedge-shaped scaut just in case the horses got harried and could not hold the waggon on the hill.

"Whatever dost want that dall great occud piece of wood for? Thee doesn't put much trust in them two 'osses. Didst see that bwoy go up ahead with the bullocks pulling his waggon as steady as a rock?"

Harry hawked and spat and between short breaths muttered, "Better be safe than sorry."

As the hill got steeper, Diamond's behaviour was exactly what might be expected of a five-year-old gelding, sleek and black, well ribbed up after the Summer's grazing. With his head nodding up and down, he dropped his flat feathered hooves with the rhythm of a pendulum but somewhat faster. His traces hitched to the shaft ferruled ends were so tight that they might have been another slender pair of shafts in front of Flower. The leather backband, looped from trace to trace, arched across the middle of his back as the traces rose, curbed only by the tightening belly band linked again to the traces just behind his forelegs. As hames tightened against collar and collar pressed on his broad chest, the two metre straps puckered where they joined the top of the hames to the fore-end of the long crupper. Here was man's best friend pulling his weight. Weighing up the situation like a mountain climber, he could occasionally feel an easement when Flower's togs pulled even harder at the front of the long staple where the ridge chain joined the shafts crossing her back in that deep furrow of the cart saddle. At the hilltop a slight pause enabled both man and beast to get their wind. Harry slipped the scaut at the back of the near back wheel and with "Hold back Flower" the togs slackened; the only weight she had was the weight of the waggon shafts across her back carried by the ridge chain. On a couple of corn sacks spread on the ground under a Cotswold stone wall, Harry and Lijah sat for a few minutes, ate bread and cheese from their frail baskets and drank cider from their costrel barrels.

Cosgrove, their destination, could hardly be described as a hamlet—just a farm and two cottages belonging to the village of Stonebow. As the little party moved off, the Cotswold plateau encouraged the horses to move at a cracking pace and once again Lijah slummocked sidesaddle on Diamond and Harry sat on the waggon. The track to Cosgrove turned sharp right through a small coppice where the stone farmhouse, the buildings, the yard and the two cottages lay in a sheltered hollow, coppice on one side, a stone quarry on the other.

The wider stony road, with well used wheel ruts, to the left led to Stonebow village a quarter of a mile away. Cosgrove farmhouse stood empty, curtainless and deserted since the Hedgecocks had left the day before. The buildings and stables were empty of cattle and horses, the implements all gone from the yard, but in the barn was a bay of wheat straw tied in boltings by straw bands, neat and tidy, then a bay of loose barley straw. Out in the rickyard, two ricks stood side by side—one of hay, one of Cotswold sanfoin, each thatched and pegged against the worst that Winter could bring—snow, rain and gales. The incoming tenant at Cosgrove would have winter fodder for his stock as George Hedgecock would at Sundial Farm. As the waggon approached this Autumn scene, the Steel and Hicks children heard the creak of the wheels, the jingle of the harness, the endless banter between Harry and Lijah and, at last, the opening of the farm gate, the bark of Lijah's cattle-dog as with wagging tail and a welcoming gleam in his eyes he went to meet his master.

Harry's wife, Esther, had had three children: Tom, a tall lad for his twelve years, David, who would be nine at Christmas, and Lucy, a sweet curly-haired four-year-old. Lijah's family, with Jane his wife, were Dick, thirteen, fat, impish and rosy-cheeked like his Dad, and Mary, eleven, brown-eyed and dark like her Mother.

Esther and Jane had stacked their worldly goods outside the front doors of the two cottages. The waggon drew up outside the garden gate and Lijah unhooked Diamond off the front end of the shafts and walked him round to the tailboard of the waggon. He tied him with a rope halter to the breach of the vehicle where the farm men early that morning had placed a kerf of hay. Harry tucked the spare rein of Flower's bridle under the chin strap and looped it over her left ear as he had so often done before. This was so that the mare, when she ate her hay from the little heap on the ground which Harry had unloaded off the waggon, should not put her front feet through the loose rein.

"It's lovely to see my man!" Jane burst into tears as she hugged Lijah when they met on the garden path. "I unt slept avout him aside a me since we walked the aisle at St Andrew's at Stonebow. Fifteen years ago, yunt it, Esther? We tied the knot the same February."

"Bless the 'ooman, thee had'st got the old dog Rough to look after tha," Lijah said as his arm wrapped her around the waist and his partly buttoned waistcoat pressed against the herden apron.

While Harry and Esther said their how-do's, the children and Rough ran in circles around the garden. The two families ate their dinner together in Harry Steel's kitchen, it being a bit larger. The fat bacon from the frail basket was shared by all and Jane Hicks tipped out a saucepan of potatoes to help fill up before the journey. Over dinner, Esther and Jane talked and reminisced as women do. "We'll miss the church at Stonebow for weddings and christenings."

"Ah," said Esther. "We a reared three and two be buried thur. Mind we could never have afforded five little uns."

"And we a reared two, despite the smallpox and diphtheria, and buried one," Jane added, cutting another piece of fat boiled bacon for Dick, "and we a got a lot to thank God for." Lijah smacked his lips over the last of the cider. Harry lit his clay pipe and looking at the cold, empty oven grate, blackleaded ready for the next farm servant, he put one hobnailed, booted foot on the fender and exclaimed, "Ar, the churchyard a bin a great blessing to us all."

"How could you be so unnatural hard!" Esther cried out. "Only think of the little uns down there. Think how Jane and me a bin through nine months a suffering for um."

" 'Tis nature," said Lijah, "we beunt all meant to live. 'Tis the same at lambing time, unt it, Harry?"

"You beunt a likening us to a couple of old yows, you heartless craters, that's enough," and with that last remark Jane fetched a pail of water from the outside pump and started washing the few crocks.

Lijah and Harry put their bags of precious taters they had grown in the garden in the bed of the waggon, then their strings of onions, harvested and dried, the beds, the chairs, the tables, all fitted into place. The crocks, ornaments and breakables were packed in sacks of straw and the whole of the loading, helped by the older children, was complete in no time. The horses were watered, hitched tandem to the waggon where the women and the children climbed aboard and made themselves comfortable on table tops and feather beds, while Lijah mounted Diamond and Harry sat at the fore end of the waggon with Rough. A picture to be sure, but a picture which could be seen every Michaelmas and every Lady Day that came round on the calendar.

"What's it like at Ayshon, Harry?" Esther whispered to her husband at the front of the waggon.

"They unt bad houses, handy the road and plenty a spring water. Lijah a got a pig sty at the back of his place, thatched an' all. Course we be only labourers like; we ain't got no strips of arable to cultivate and grow a bit of corn for ourselves. We a got no grazing rights on the common. You never see such lands, ridge and furrow like they be at Ayshon. If you stands in the bottom a one open furrow, the land is ridged up so high that you can't see the man in the next furrow. The ridges be small, mind, some unt a third of an acre. They have all got the telltale twist anant the headland where the bullocks start to turn afore they gets to the end of the furrow. Ayshon folks got thur arable strips along Beckford way, that's the Tewkesbury road, and some more along Staights Furlong towards the old castle ruin at Elmley Gorse, but the best ground, they says, is the strips in the Groaten towards Carrants Brook. They mows good crops down thur, not like up yer where the grass don't hardly hide a hare in June. The common grazings be on Bredon Hill, where thur's plenty of spring water too, they do say, and that's apart from a bit of enclosure made some years back. Our gaffer's place is enclosed but he a got grazing rights."

The waggonload of furniture and the two labouring families soon came to the steep descent of Stanway Hill. Lijah and Harry dismounted from their horse and waggon, put the lock chain through the spokes of the lefthand wheel, slid the skid pan under the iron tyre of the wheel and holding their horses with Flower's summerfat ass pushing back against the wide breeching strap as she dug her hind feet in the worn track, the waggon descended comfortably down the hill, with Diamond's traces slack and swinging from side to side as he walked quite independent of the waggon. The boys pulled horse-chestnuts off the overhanging trees and grabbed handfuls of beechmast and acorns still in their cups, while the girls were content with the odd blackberry when the transport passed a narrow gap in the bushes. Lijah and Harry had brought back with them from Cosgrove some wooden blocks for the fire grates at Ayshon, a few gorse faggots to fire the bread oven. Right from the time they were toddlers, the Steels' and the Hickses' children had been encouraged to forage. "Forage for anything," Lijah and Harry said, "blackberries, mushrooms, but mind whose land you be on."

At the edge of night, after one of the last days in September, the two families arrived at their black and white cottages in Ayshon. They unloaded their goods, had an evening meal by fire and candle light and Lijah once more lay with Jane on the oatchaff-filled bed tick. Esther lay once more by her Harry, and beneath the stars, with the hooting of the owls nearby, the occasional bark of a dog fox and the scream of the vixen, Ayshon, or most of Ayshon, was asleep too.

Early next morning Harry Steel tied up the milking cows in the long shed at Sundial Farm. Wearing his battered greasy hat, coated with cow hair, and seated on a three-legged stool, a wooden pail between his legs, and sitting, as always, on the right side, he drove his head hard into the cow's flanks and started milking. With her two front teats in his experienced hands, the milk flowed. As he alternated to her hind teats, the familiar chee-chaw-chee-chaw sounded in the bottom of the pail. George Hedgecock had only brought ten milk cows with him, his ten best. The low yielders and the kickers had gone to Haverford market.

Harry soon finished milking and as he delivered the milk to the dairy, Anne Hedgecock made preparations there for butter and cheese making. Lijah fed the young cattle in the yard, starting a cut of hay from the new rick in the yard left by the outgoing tenant. Flower and Diamond were fed, the gaffer's hunter and Mark's pony. After breakfast that morning, George Hedgecock took Lijah to the wheat stubble field enclosed near the villagers' strips at Staights Furlong. Two teams were ploughing the ridges on some of Staights Furlong's strips. Each plough was pulled by four horses at length, or four horses walking in line up the furrow. The ploughmen were accompanied by ploughboys with long leather whips which they cracked as they swung their short wooden whip sticks. The long wooden wheel-less ploughs pushed the heavy loam up the steep slopes of the lands, turning the golden stubble to a lightish brown as furrow followed furrow up and down the strip field.

"Stop a minute, my good man," George said to one of the ploughmen as his boy turned the horses on the headland. "You're a smallholder, no doubt?"

"I be," replied Abel Smith. "I've only got three-quarters of an acre, that's two ridged up lands. I must a' me time work for the Reverend Philip Besford, these be his horses. 'Course I got grazing rights for a cow, a pig and a few geese on the common. That's a mate a mine yonder, he's Fred Pickford. That's Master Bosworth's team he's ploughing with, he's a three-quarter of an acre man like me, they be Bosworth's horses. We should turn our stint over today, then back ploughing for the Gaffer to-morrow. You see this ground wants the Winter frost to lax it afore we plants our Spring barley."

George Hedgecock turned to Lijah, kicked the fresh-turned furrow and said at once, "This is not Cotswold ground, Diamond and Flower won't pull a long wooden plough through this land." Abel Smith said, as he leaned heavily on his plough tails, "Hol-brook is just as heavy as this is, it's four horse land. Squire

Waterford's men ploughs with bullocks on the enclosure a' top a
Bredon Hill. Mind, it's lighter up there.''

"Call at the dairy tomorrow morning, Abel, before you go to
work," said George Hedgecock, "and I'll give you a drink of
cider.''

Abel, who had to be at Besford's stable by six, called at
Sundial Farm at just turned five the next morning. Mrs Hedgecock
was working with Catherine and Tilda, as they called her, in the
dairy. Abel was heartened to see such activity. He worked for a
retired parson's wife. "Nice to see a 'ooman with her sleeves
turned up past her elbows at five o'clock in the morning. You'll
do well at Sundial and this drop of cider is kind to the belly this
morning." "You are welcome, Abel, I'm glad we met." George
Hedgecock really meant this. He added, "You see, if I had sent
Lijah to plough Holbrook with two horses, a pretty fool we
should have all looked. I shall have to buy two more to plough
that sort of land.''

It being Wednesday, George Hedgecock and Lijah urgently
went to Tewkesbury market. George sent Lijah on ahead, riding
Diamond sidesaddle along Beckford way, and giving him half an
hour's start, saddled his hunter and followed, catching him up at
Hardwicke, three miles short of Tewkesbury. At the market the
horses paraded up Barton Street with plaited manes beribboned as
dealers with long whips put them through their paces over
cobbled streets. "Don't thee be ginled by their finery, Gaffer,
you wants two sound in wind and limb.''

"All right, Lijah, we will watch points awhile," his boss replied.

Outside one of the pubs, a decent sort of fellow, not a horse
coper or dealer, but a man who bred, reared and broke horses,
had two liver chestnut mares five years old, each standing sixteen
and a half hands, quiet and in good condition. George looked
them over, felt down their legs for side bones, under their

crupper for sweet itch, ran at their wide chests with his fist as
if to hit them to see if they were roarers or weak in the windpipe.
"What work have they done?" he enquired then of the owner.
"They have worked well in chains. I've not tried them in shafts
but they are quiet honest workers on the plough." "How
much?" said George Hedgecock, and after much banter George
and the owner beat the palms of their right hands together and
shouted "Sold" for all and sundry to hear so that there could be
no comeback. Lijah haltered the first mare, tying the loose end to
Diamond's tail, tied the second mare to the other's tail, then
mounted Diamond and, head to tail, the team made for Ayshon.
George Hedgecock, pleased with his purchase, trotted over track
and bridlepath back to Sundial Farm.

George Hedgecock soon got Lijah started with his, now, four-
horse team, ploughing Holbrook. Tom Steel drove the team as
ploughboy. It was strange for Lijah at first, ploughing the land in
unbroken stretch furrow, turning it, knit together, like bacon
rashers. The Cotswold limestone land fell to pieces as it was
ploughed and a light harrowing produced a seed bed.

While Tom Steel whistled his day away, walking on the un-
ploughed stubble, cracking his whip and talking to the team,
Lijah wrestled with his great wooden plough as he waddled up
the furrow. He had put Flower as filler (or thriller)—the horse
at the rear hitched directly onto the plough. His only way of
controlling the depth of his furrow was by raising or lowering
the traces as the length of the ridge chain crossing the filler's
back, through the slot in the cart saddle, was adjusted. Of course,
by bearing heavily on the plough tails, or handles, the share dug
shallower into the soil, and by carrying the plough tails, or tilt-
ing them slightly, the iron point of the share attached to the
shield board, or mould board, penetrated deeper into the sub-
soil. Diamond was his foremost horse, a big strapping gelding,

needed in front to pull up rather than down on the collars of the two five-year-old mares in the middle— the body horse and the lash horse; Lijah had named them Daisy and Dolly. "They be shaping well, Gaffer, a bit green, sweats smartish, but they ull come to," was the carter's opinion.

George Hedgecock had worked the land and travelled in the Vale country long enough to know that the Winter frosts would lax and crumble Holbrooks clay. Meanwhile Harry had his cows to milk and his yearlings to feed, and as George had grazing rights on Bredon Hill common, he bought a small flock of ewes and turned them up there. Lord Waterford had already overstocked the hill with his sheep— the ewes and rams ran the hill together. The Hedgecocks also turned out sows in the Ayshon Wood, together with those of other villagers who had grazing rights to do so. These all ran with a boar pig, the property of Stephen Bosworth, tenant on part of Lord Waterford's estate.

Harry with his cattle- and sheep-dog, Rough, kept a careful eye on Hedgecock's cattle, sheep and pigs, envying somewhat his neighbours who had rights to keep a pig or cow on the common. There were thirty families with a small acreage of arable and grazing rights on the common. The bigger farmers were Lord Waterford himself, who leased a part of his estate to Stephen Bosworth, the Rev. Philip Besford, a retired village parson, and George Hedgecock, tenant to Lady Sarah Fitzwilliam who lived at the Old Manor and retained two small paddocks of land. Lord Waterford, being the real Lord of the Manor, lived at Beckford Hall. Archdeacon Trusswell, although he held the living at several parishes, had put in curates in charge and lived himself at Beckford vicarage, farming his forty acres of glebe at Ayshon. There were about forty labourers like Harry and Lijah who worked full time on their masters' farms.

The Steel and Hicks children took notice of their parents'

abbit Lane wattle and daub cottages at Beckford.

Cross Barn Cross, Ayshon.

A Meet in the Park, the county's upper crust leading the pack.

instruction and foraged for acorns, beechmast, crab apples, sloes and all the crops of the hedges and the open fields. The dry acorns and beechmast were stored, great ketchup mushrooms from Bredon Hill were turned into ketchup, and Esther and Jane spun the wool the families gathered off blackthorn and gorse on the common land and woodland.

The Cottagers' Pig

Just before Christmas 1768 Harry Steel on his rounds found one of Mr Hedgecock's sows had farrowed in the wood. All the piglets were dead under a blackberry bush which was bowed down by an early fall of snow. This was a young gilt pig, her first litter, and she looked too weak to get up from her leafy bed. Down at Sundial, the gaffer told Harry to take Diamond with Lijah, put a bolting of straw on a farm gate and drag the young sow back to the buildings. In a loose box next to calf pens the young sow gained enough strength, after a drink of warm skimmed milk, to raise herself to her feet. What a spectacle she looked. "Backbone sharp as a razor," Lijah commented, and "Nothing but skin and bone," said George Hedgecock. Mrs Hedgecock said she would have looked after her but just hadn't the time.

"Her ull never stand to boar again," added Lijah.

"No good wasting time looking at her. Put her in your sty, Lijah," said George. "You and Harry can have her between you and the missus will let you have some skimmed milk until she improves."

Not since their wedding day had Lijah or Harry had a pig of their own. The whole family sat up all night with the young sow, warming skimmed milk, tempting her with crushed apples, turnip and a saucepan of taters.

"I allus reckons as thurs nothing like bacon from a sow as have had one bellyful a pigs. Once they starts to put on flesh they fattens quicker than anything as I knows too. I a bin given some of the bacon and the fat's about three inches thick then just a streak of lean. My eyes, Harry, we be going to be lucky for once."

"Don't count your chickens yet," Harry said, "but our womenfolk won't let that un die in the sty. Women be more patient uth weaklings than what thee and me be."

Of course the sow lived and thrived on skimmed milk and acorns, beechmast and all the good things the Hickses and Steels could provide.

Christmas came to Ayshon and Harry and Lijah's families got to know some of the village families — the Bradfields, the Winnets, the Allens, who met them at the Plough on Saturday nights. They heard from them of older days in Ayshon. Some could remember 1729 when forty-five people died suddenly of swellings of the throat between January and May — more folks, it was said, than all the twenty years before. Then there was the landslide of 1764, only four years ago, when the footpath to Beckford slipped seventy yards overnight down Bredon Hill according to Berrow's *Worcester Journal*. "Mind, it's in the parish records," said Job Allen, "that some of the hobbledehoys got a playing cudgels in the churchyard about 1635 after the vicar had warned us against Sunday sports and dall me if one on 'em didn't have his eye cut out as clear as a whistle."

"It don't pay to trifle with the Almighty," Jim Bradfield spluttered out, blowing the froth off his mug of beer all over Bernard Baker's clean smock frock. "No he beunt to be trifled with."

When Sam Parson recalled the last public execution at A'sum in 1744, Harry and Lijah looked at one another, thinking all the time we shan't have to put a foot wrong or else we shall be for the high jump. "It was a Beckford girl, a dissenter married at twenty to an A'sum maltster, her name was Liz Owen and she married a chap named Moreton."

"Her was but a child," said old Jim Bradfield, "and her got some poison from an apothecary's shop at A'sum. Her bloke was older and her poisoned him. They hung, drawed and quartered her top at Greenhill, her was in the family way and her confessed in the cart on the way there from Worcester Castle. A bloody job I called it—not a using any oaths, but no doubt her mind was upset."

"What's old Archdeacon Trusswell like?" asked Lijah, who was anxious to know what sort of parson he had got.

"A haristocrak," Bernard Baker described him. "He got a coachman, you'll see the coach coming, cockade and all. He's chairman at the Sessions, no mercy with his justice. Still, it pays to hold the candle to him, don't it, Jim." Jim Bradfield roused from his doze in front of the log fire, said "Oi," and then dozed again.

"How's the sow a going you two Cotswold men a got?" Sam Parson was interested.

"Half fat, unt she, Lijah?" Harry replied. "I reckon her ull make twenty score by Candlemas then we'll have her in salt."

Hunting on Bredon Hill

That Winter, meets of the harriers, the huntsmen in their green jackets, were often held at Ayshon Manor where Lady Sarah was hostess, and at Beckford Hall, Squire Lord Waterford's place. Hares abounded on Bredon Hill, and men like George Hedgecock and young Mark followed on their horses. The Rev. Philip Besford turned out too on these occasions, Stephen Bosworth and his wife, and many more farmers from around the hill. The flat top of Bredon Hill was more suitable for hare hunting than hunting the fox; hares circle on their own territory and are loath to run straight with the wind like a fox. The cry of "ant, ant, ant" as the hounds caught the warmed hare with her ears laid and putting her last ounce into the chase, was common.

Over the other side of Bredon Hill, over the river past Eckington, Lord Coventry lived with young Lady Coventry at his Tudor mansion at Earls Broughton. He erected a Folly at Caperlea at the end of a mile long avenue of trees, just to please her Ladyship. Lord Coventry owned estates all around Bredon Hill; his grounds, folks said, were the work of the great landscape gardener, Capability Brown. He ran two packs of foxhounds and hunted on Bredon Hill; they met at Beckford Hall and Lord and Lady Waterford hunted with them. After hospitality at the Hall, the pack moved up Bredon Hill, past the washpool and the firs to draw Beckford Coppice. Lord Coventry was a man of twenty-five, his wife, newly married to him, was twenty-two. Lord and Lady Waterford were some fifteen years older, both keen riders to hounds. Lord Waterford had inherited the estate on his father's death about four years earlier. Beckford Coppice was drawn by the hounds and they drew a blank. The county's upper crust led the pack with Lord Coventry as Master. His two Whips following were the Rev. Philip Besford and Stephen Bosworth, with George Hedgecock on his heavy hunter and Mark on his pony bringing up the rear. Harry Steel agreed with the system. "Parson only said in church last wick, we be to keep to our proper stations."

Harry had been sent early to the hill to help with the earth stopping to prevent reynard from going to ground. Spring Hill produced a fox—"a hell of a big dog," Harry said as he watched both the hunt and the stock being scattered by the hounds. As he stood on a knolp with his back against a beech tree, the fox had broken cover half a mile away at Spring Hill Firs, and going with his brush carried straight, the south-west wind behind him, he passed within twenty yards of Harry, who gave the "View halloa". The music of the pack as they left the firs, the baying of the first few couples when they got a scent, frightened Harry's flock of sheep, but soon the hounds were following the contour of the hill as they made after the fox to Ayshon Wood.

Lord Waterford rode with his wife. They knew Bredon Hill well, knew the bridle gate where the enclosure ended. Lord Coventry's iron grey gelding foamed and lathered as he rode side by side with his First Whip close behind the hounds. The locals knew the hill pretty well but Harry had yet to realise which way the fox would take to the cover of Ayshon Wood. He followed the huntsmen, climbing the occasional stone wall or forcing his way through bramble and gorse. He walked down Furze Hill, the hill where the men with Common Rights could cut faggots for heating their bread ovens. A lone figure passed him on a liver chestnut. Her immaculate riding habit told Harry that the side-saddled rider was no ordinary follower of hounds. He touched his hat. "Good morning, Marm."

"Good morning," Lady Coventry replied. "Could you tell me the line to take to Ayshon Wood cover?"

"Sorry, marm, I don't know this hill very well. I only come down off the Cotswolds at Christmas."

"My husband runs a pack up there too," she said with a girlish twinkle in her eye.

She cantered across the hill towards an old enclosure known as the Cuckoo Pen. The wall on Beckford side was standing three feet high above a springy wild thyme covered turf. Nothing has ever been created to excel the beauty of a real liver chestnut hunter, groomed and got up for hunting by grooms and strappers

in stables such as were at Earls Broughton. This was matched by
Lady Coventry herself; her poise, the way she sat her horse.
Then, seeing the rest of the hunt and the pack skirting Shaw
Green coppice and the wood in the background, she put her
horse confidently at the stone wall and with an "Up my girl!"
cleared it beautifully.

On the other side of the wall the ground dropped steeply into
a disused quarry and horse and rider fell twelve feet head
first into it. The mare's back broke as she fell on her knees
pitching its rider over her head into the quarry. Paralysed, the
mare lay still on its side, helpless and hopeless. Lady Coventry
got up on to one knee but found she had badly sprained one ankle
and was quite unable to walk. By now, the hunt had taken its fox
through Ayshon Wood towards Elmley Castle. His Lordship
knew nothing of the accident. Then Harry arrived, saw the
plight of horse and rider, saw Lady Coventry crying on the grass
because she had lost her best hunter.

"Never you mind, my dear," Harry, though only in his
thirties, spoke in a fatherly way. "I'll soon get you down the
hill to Ayshon."

"What about my lovely mare?" Lady Coventry sobbed.

"The gaffer ull see to her later. Her unt in no pain, her's
paralysed."

Lady Coventry put her right arm round Harry's neck and
Harry put his arm around her waist and led her to a low part of
the wall. Then, as if he was picking up a child's doll, he gently
lifted her onto the wall. "I'll take you down on my back now,
your Ladyship. First let me take your riding boot off afore your
ankle swells too bad."

"You are so kind, my man, how can I repay you?" Lady
Coventry whispered hoarsely. This made drops of sweat fall from
Harry's nose.

"Now stand against my back, put one leg over my one shoulder, then I'll help you to get the bad one over the other, and you can hold my neck with both hands and ride cock-a-lantern down to Lady Sarah's at the Old Manor."

She sat on Harry's shoulders as light as a feather to him while he steadied her with his hands just above her knees. He had put her one riding boot into his frail basket, which also hung from his shoulder. As the road was steep and stony down the close at the back of the church, Lady Coventry's soft gloved hands gripped Harry's neck and Harry held tighter to her knees. As Harry's heart made his blood surge through his veins, his head went muzzy and he felt about ten feet tall. The colour came red and then purple to his cheeks and he admitted that the Old Manor came far too soon. He was momentarily in fairyland—the young wife of a Lord riding cock-a-lantern on his back! He would dream of it for years to come.

Lady Sarah, with the help of her maids, bound up her Ladyship's ankle. Esther, who soon heard of the accident, called at the Manor to help.

"What can I give your husband for his kindness?" Lady Coventry asked Esther.

"Well, we 'ave got a pig and we could do with some barley to finish fattening him."

"You shall have some next week for certain," said Lady Coventry. Meanwhile Lady Sarah arranged a carriage to take the invalid home.

"Before I go," Lady Coventry told Harry, "see that my mare is painlessly put down."

What a day for Harry to remember—and the bag of barley duly came. "It's an ill wind as blows nobody any good," he told Lijah that night.

The Steels and the Hickses shared and shared alike. The barley that came from Lady Coventry was sparingly fed with the offal from the swill tub to the fattening sow. When February and Candlemas came, Lijah gave the sow her last breakfast and just an evening drink of water. Lijah Hicks had learned from his old Dad how to kill a pig and the following morning, before work started at Sundial Farm, Harry, Lijah, Fred Pickford and Abel Smith laid the fat squealing sow on George Hedgecock's pig bench and as the saying goes 'death was almost instantaneous'.

Now for the burning—quite an art this. "You got to take account of the wind," Lijah told his helpers. A bolting of wheat straw was spread all over the sow, now motionless on the Hickses' garden path. Straw was shoved under her tail, straw was placed in her open mouth and with her tail towards the wind, Lijah lit up and very soon the fire was burning the bristles off the pig's shins as it worked its way up from the sow's rear. Lijah parted the bolting with a short iron shuppick; this kept the fire moving so that no part of the pig's skin would be burnt. Then Harry turned the sow on her back and pitched more straw onto her upturned belly until the whole of the pig showed black in the firelight. A sharp twist on each cloven hoof took the half burned horny part away from the trotters underneath. Lijah threw these half-baked hooves to Rough the dog who ate them with relish.

"Thur's no waste to a pig," Lijah reminded the group. "You can eat it all except the squeal." With a stiff broom Harry swept all the burnt straw and the burnt stubble of sow's hair off the carcase and then, back on the bench, buckets of cold water, buckets of hot water and buckets of lukewarm water were slushed over the Hickses' and Steels' windfall. Lijah got busy with a scrubbing brush at one end and Harry at the other until the whole thing was spotless and white except for a few hairs which had escaped the fire. These Harry shaved off with the skill of a city barber. Then Lijah paunched the sow while the women waited with salt glazed crock bowls to receive the liver, the lights, the chitterlings and all that goes to make up a pig. Two of George Hedgecock's hooks were then inserted into the place only a pig killer would know where to find—at the rear of the sow. These hooks were joined by a strong cord.

"Now you chaps, now's the time we wants some help. I wants her slung across that beam in the shed anant the sty."

The men lifted the carcase towards the door and Lijah slung the rope across the beam. "Now her up," and each time they lifted, Lijah tightened the rope across the beam, bringing the ass end of the pig closer to the beam, and there she hung, her snout about a foot from the ground. Harry cut a nut stick in the garden hazel bush, pointed its ends with his knife and, while Lijah stood there holding the pig's apron or stomach lining in both hands, Harry prised her two loins apart to let in the cold fresh air, put in the stick, and then Lijah professionally threw the apron over the front legs of the creature.

"That's it for this morning, chaps, we'll divide her tomorrow night when hers set well." The women got busy with the offal, cleaning the chitterlings, and dividing the liver, but the family waited one more day before they tasted pig meat, when plates of tit bits were sent round by the children to the Pickfords and Smiths for their help.

"When them two sides of bacon be salted, I be looking forward to seeing a picture on thy wall and another on mine," Harry said. "Them be the pictures you wants when you be a family man."

Her Ladyship and Esther

Tom Steel worked as ploughboy to Lijah Hicks and Dick Hicks

found work as under cowman for the Rev. Philip Besford. This meant that with Harry and Lijah each earning around six shillings a week, the boys' money helped to keep things going. It was a hard life for Jane and Esther—having rights on the common would have made it easier—but George Hedgecock was a good master. Anne, his wife, gave milk from the Hedgecock dairy for the family in times of sickness. The labouring families lived mostly on bread and potatoes, turnips and the allowance of cider from the Master. Rabbits from the hill quite often found their way into the frail basket, though Lord Waterford, the squire, and Archdeacon Trusswell, the vicar, would soon send any offending villager to Gloucester Castle or prison for as much as poaching. The Archbishop of Canterbury and six of his bishops had even voted in the Lords against abolishing the death penalty for stealing as little as five shillings, but the Member of Parliament for Worcester was a champion of the poor, and so was the good Lord Coventry, who declared that a parson who farmed his glebe in the week was a better parson on Sunday. Fred Pickford, who had a large family to keep on Bosworth's pittance, used to say, "Better to poach and be hanged than see the little uns starve."

Such was life in Ayshon: Lady Sarah a kindly woman, the Squire and the Archdeacon completely heartless; the Rev. Philip Besford helpful to the poor; Stephen Bosworth, although a tenant to Lord Waterford, autocratic and mean. The ladies were kinder and more sympathetic but subject to the menfolk. The Wardens, the parish roundsmen, were continually on the look out for women coming into the parish and giving birth to bastards the parish had to keep.

Lady Coventry never forgot Harry Steel's kindness and took young David, when he was ten, into her mansion as house boy. Then one day she rode over to Ayshon to see Esther. She wanted to start a family, but still wanted to hunt, to dance, to lead the social life expected of a lady of her standing.

"Have you and Harry thought of having any more children, Esther?" she asked.

"Well, now we a got young David and Tom at work, no doubt we could manage another; why, your Ladyship?"

"Would you mind having two on the breast at once, Esther?— I mean would you feed one for me?"

"Yes, I'll do that. I'm sure Harry would be proud of me. He's never finished talking about carrying you down Bredon Hill."

Esther was not the sort of woman that could be met any day. Harry always said, "She has her babbies like shelling peas from a pod—no fuss, no bother." She was a buxom woman compared with Harry's angular figure. He reckoned that way back she had come of Romany stock. With her black hair, her ample bosom, her wide hips and strong arms that pulled the rake at haymaking and loaded the sheaves at harvest, she was a fine figure of a countrywoman.

"Think you'll give birth to another child, Esther? You're thirty-two, aren't you?"

"Lor' bless your Ladyship, our Harry only got to lie close to me and I be in the family way. It's like that with some folks, ent it?"

When Lady Coventry had gone, Harry came in for his evening meal and Esther told him the news. That night Harry planted seed with Esther long before the ground had dried for the barley planting. Lord and Lady Coventry would be expecting a happy event, as they put it in their circles, just before the opening meet of the fox hounds in November.

"Oh hoy," said Fred Pickford (or was it the beer that talked at the Plough a few Saturday nights after?). "Thur's many a poor girl as laughs on Good Friday but urs a crying come Boxing Day."

"It unt like that," Abel Smith belched over his pint. "These youngsters be planned for."

"Planned for!" Fred roared with laughter. "Ourn come—planned or no. Lust the parson calls it, I calls it nature."

Fred Pickford's eldest boys, who both worked for the Squire, listened to their elders. They were twins, Reuben and Amos, and in their teens. "Dad," Reuben said, "Why is it that Lady Coventry a got to have a wet nurse?" "It's like this bwoy." Fred heaved himself a bit more upright in his chair to explain a tricky question. "Lady Coventry a got appearances to keep up—hunt balls, parties, hunting, shooting along of the Lord. Her can't suckle a youngster." Abel Smith, another staid son of the Ayshon soil, added, "Now, Reuben, you helps along a the squire's cows, you 'a sin a heifer calve down with the tits on her bag firm and straight, thee ast also sin an old cow with her bag amus dragging the ground on account of being sucked and bunted by calves time and time agun." "That's just how it is with women," Fred Pickford added. "Esther's tits, if you notice, be hangin' like a couple of mella pears, almost to her waist. It's natur, Harry don't mind, but it's different with the gentry, they corsets themselves in place. It udn't look right at the Hunt Ball if they didn't, but for the likes a we it don't matter, do it, Abel?" Abel lit his clay pipe with a wooden spill from the fire and chuckled as he said, "That unt all a the story. Esther 'a got gipsy blood in her, her 'ull have plenty a milk, thee ut see. Like enough 'er Ladyship udn't have enough to rear a kitten and they tells me the gentry sends out cocoa to them as wet nurses, that's the tack um reckons to make milk. Then a course Mrs Hedgecock will have orders to provide plenty of cows' milk for the Steels."

Fred Pickford sat back and thought of the children Emma Pickford had had, some she had reared, others they had lost.

"I'll be dalled if I don't wish our Emma was young enough to have two in bed with her. Still, I'd sooner father all me own. What dost thee say, Abel?" "They do say if the good Lord knowed of anything better, he kept it to himself. Mind, we shouldn't begrudge Harry all the benefits he's a gwain to have seeing as he carried her Ladyship down Bredon Hill." "Carried her Ladyship down Bredon Hill!" Fred cleared his throat and spat in the fire. "Harry enjoyed every minute of that, he told me her had a nice pair of shafts. I suppose we shouldn't talk a women like this, but 'tis natur."

CHAPTER TWO

First Spring and Summer at Sundial Farm

Countryfolk at market.

The farmer's boy with his thumb bit of bread and cheese.

Lady Day 1769

THE FROSTS and drying winds of late Winter had made a tilth as fine as sugar out of the stiff clay of Ayshon, both on the small arable strips of the smallholders, Autumn ploughed by the squire's men and the farmers' men, and on the land farmed by the Rev. Philip Besford. When Lady Day arrived two more families came to Ayshon village. They found the land in good heart and fit for sowing; they found the livestock improving every day as the nights grew shorter and sweet fresh grass sprouted on sunny banks.

To Bumbow, a little holding of orchard, paddock and yard, thatched black and white half timbered, half wattle and daub house, the Rev. Richard Surman came straight from the University of Oxford. Archdeacon Trusswell had appointed him his curate. He brought with him his widowed mother. His father, a doctor of medicine in Oxford, had died two years before. The Archdeacon who lived at Beckford had several parishes under his care, besides being Chairman of the Magistrates at Beckford Court. "The old man Trusswell have often told us," Fred Pickford remarked over his quart at the Plough, "that many are called but few are chosen. Whether it be an honour to be chose by the Archdeacon or no remains to be proved."

The other family to join the natives under the shelter of Bredon Hill were Francis Stokes, his wife Honour, both around thirty years of age, young Andrew, their eight-year-old boy and his sister Elizabeth, six last Christmas. Their role in village life would be very important, for Francis, who had crossed the River Avon from Upton, had been appointed Bailiff, or as the locals preferred 'Bailey', to Lord Waterford.

The house and yard of Cullabine House had housed many
bailiffs before. The last one, an old man named Hobbins, had
been stricken with illness and old age and had moved to his son's
little farm at Elmley Castle at Candlemas.

Lady Day, 25th March, meant long hours for Harry Steel as
stockman to George Hedgecock. Lambing was well under way
on Bredon Hill and Harry's very being felt at home nine hundred
odd feet above sea level. It was just about at the same height as
he had been at Cosgrove over on the Cotswolds and every morning when the sky was clear he saw the sun rise over those hills—
those ten-mile-away hills which looked so near on days when
rain was about and which appeared as silhouettes when storms
sweeping up the Severn Vale almost hid them. Hills, thought
Harry, it's hill country that I like. A wet night in Ayshon village
and the sugary mould of the arable clung to the boots, while on
the plain of Bredon's summit, the limestone rock was near the
surface and the land, instead of being a drag to the feet of the
walker, was covered with springy turf.

Hedgecock's Cotswold type ewes benefited by the change of
pasture and that Spring gave a good fall of lambs. Harry almost
lived up there. He slept most nights in a thatched cabin amongst
the beech trees. His wood fire under a stone wall gave him
warmth after a regular walk among the folded ewes with his horn
lantern to light his way and his old dog to keep him company,
then another short sleep until he heard the unmistakable bleat of
a lambing ewe. In no time at all he would be with her; perhaps
the lamb's one front leg was folded back and she couldn't move
it; perhaps the lamb's head was back in the ewe's passage;
perhaps the hind legs were coming first. Harry had righted all
these things so many times before, he knew just what to do.
On the fire under the wall he kept an iron pot of water heated
ready for such an emergency. With his crook he caught the ewe

and brought her in to the small fold near his cabin, then, according to how difficult the birth looked, he acted in one of two ways. A leg back just meant that after opening the ewe's passage with his hands, his sleeves rolled back to his elbow and his hands and arms lathered with hot soapy water off the fire, he lambed the ewe with no fuss, no bother. In more serious cases he slung the ewe by her hind legs with plough lines to the beam in the lean-to against his thatched hut. This gave him more room to turn the lamb inside the ewe, and using plenty of soap and water and green oils to form a lubricant, he usually saved both ewe and lamb. If the operation was too painful to the ewe, Harry gave her a stiff dose of laudanum.

If the mother was not strong enough to stand and suckle her new born lamb, Harry milked her into a basin and then bottle-fed the lamb, often using a hollow elder branch, one with the pith taken out leaving a small tube which he used as a teat to dribble a little milk into the lamb's mouth. This was just an everyday and everynight duty of Harry's.

When he could leave his flock he came down to the village, to his black and white cottage, and restocked with food to take back on the hill. As he lambed George Hedgecock's ewes, he often thought of Esther. When he had one with a big udder of milk he smiled, thinking of Esther's capacity for milk and wondering how the seed he had planted long before and the seed Lord Coventry had planted in his beautiful young wife would be growing, and when he curled up on his straw mattress in his cabin for the odd midnight hour nap, he dreamed of Esther sleeping alone on her tick of oat chaff under the thatch that had kept off the rain and the sun since Queen Elizabeth rode from Elmley Castle to Sudeley Castle. "It's not good for man to live alone," old Trusswell said in church, but then didn't he quote what suited him?

"I wonder how Lijah is getting on," Harry thought. "He and Master Hedgecock ull have the cows to milk while I'm up yer."

Harry had never met Francis Stokes until, one fine morning at the end of March, Francis rode his stiff cob across Bredon Hill common and found Harry tending his flock like another David, calling each one by name. Francis was impressed by Harry's shepherding and the number of lambs he had so far reared. "Lord Waterford's flock are off the hill and Shepherd Bosley is lambing down in the Saltway Barn," said Francis, adding, "Bosley's not had a deal of experience. Would you mind looking in when you next go down to the village?— Maybe you could give him a tip or two." Harry was quite heartened to hear this from the new Bailey and he agreed to look in at Saltway Barn.

While the Stokes family settled in at Cullabine, the Rev. Richard Surman and his mother were getting straight at Bumbow. The Rev. Surman preached at St Andrew's at Ayshon on Sundays, the villagers preferring him to the autocratic Archdeacon Trusswell. As a doctor's son, Surman had more sympathy with the poor of the parish. Archdeacon Trusswell had his coach and four horses kept at Beckford vicarage and looked after by his coachman. The cockade could be seen as his reverence was driven from parish to parish in his four in hand; Ayshon was indeed fortunate to have a curate like Richard Surman.

As the hemlock grew on the banks of the ditches, the damsons in the vale, viewed from Harry's hill, appeared as driven snow, the turnips which had wintered in the ground sprouted green, and the whole natural world burst into life, farming went apace. Lijah Hicks's team of horses harrowed in the barley sowed broadcast by George Hedgecock and Mark, and the drying winds and the sun pleased George Hedgecock. Bernard Baker, Jim Bradfield, Job Allen and the other strip holders sowed their barley, weeded their winter sown wheat, ploughed back the fallow and grazed their individual cows up the village street where the grass grew early on sheltered verges.

Abel Smith planted the Rev. Philip Besford's barley, gave the outlying cows on the Leasow Common a little less hay and put sittings of thirteen eggs under each of the broody hens. He broke in a four year chain horse to work as a filler in shafts and told the reverend gentleman that the cider in the cellar was getting low. One would almost think that, at least in Ayshon in the Spring of 1769, that God was in his heaven and all was right with the world.

March is a hungry month on the land. The grass has grown enough to put the horses off their hay but is insufficient to satisfy them. Squire Waterford's oxen, which he worked on the enclosure on the south side of Bredon hill, harrowed in the oats on the untouched furrow. Harry Holmes fed them well with turnips and corn besides their hay. They were six years old and would have to make beef in the Summer. Harry Holmes was a young strong man of twenty, the eldest of a large family, living with his mother and crippled father. When he stole potatoes from his employer, Lord Waterford, Francis Stokes was duty bound to inform him about it and Harold was brought before the Archdeacon at Beckford Court. He sentenced him to be publicly whipped, tied to a cart next Tewkesbury Market Day from the Swan to the Black Bull and back. This was a duty performed by the public hangman before a large crowd. Seventeen shillings and sixpence was collected for the hangman. Harold returned to Ayshon with his stripes.

Bernard Baker told the company in the Plough that night: "I a lived in this parish man and bwoy since me old Mother gin birth to ma at Camp House, the house on Bredon Hill wur Old Cromwell s'posed to a tied his oss during the Civil War . . .

but I've overrun me tale. It's sixty-five years last November since I saw the light.'' Bernard continued his tale to his cider-sodden, open-mouthed commoners, all younger men.

"My old grandfather was parish clerk yer for sixty years, he continued in office until he was ninety, coming to the church on two sticks—too weak to feed himself so he had to be fed with a spoon. He studied the records in the church chest and about two hundred year ago William Hicks of Ayshon confessed to impregnating Ann Jinks. The words says in black and white that he had carnal knowledge with her.''

"I can't think a no better,'' Sam Parsons butted in.

"Ah,'' Bernard said as he put his mug down on the fireside settle, '' 'tis alright for the gentry but not for the likes a we. Hicks made two journeys to Tewkesbury and one to Winchcombe on account of his sin. 'Dressed in a white robe' the record says. He confessed at Tewkesbury Market a the Wednesday, Winchcombe market a the Saturday, then again at Tewkesbury Abbey a the Sunday, saying he had offended God and was sorry for it. Then about nine years afore that, Henry Hynds was excommunicated for denying the power of the Church.''

Bernard added, "My brother Charles is still Clerk to the Archdeacon and mind ya, Charles is crafty—he don't only hold the candle in church, he has to hold the candle for him time and time again.''

The company at the Plough sat in awe at Bernard's tales, knowing that the Baker family had lived at Ayshon for four hundred years and had held office as Clerk as a matter of course. Then the conversation turned to enclosure. Away back in 1701 Lady Sarah's grandfather, Sir George Woolass, and Lord Waterford's grandfather, the old Lord Waterford, had made an attempt at enclosing all the common land. This was never implemented apart from the enclosed farms of the squire, the parson and Lady

Sarah. The thought of the commoners losing their strips for corn growing, their right of grazing a cow, a few geese and in some cases a horse on Bredon Hill, the right to cut furze for firing their bread ovens on that rabbit-infested waste of Furze Hill, didn't bear thinking about. They would become common labourers and wouldn't it be better to follow the dictates of squire and parson and keep that little bit of independence that their fathers and their ancestors had held so dear?

Spring Sowing

As the white blossom of the blackthorn was blown away by the showers and winds of April, the elder showed its leaves of palest green, flat bushes of blackberry on Bredon Hill burst into bud, the may trees gave Ayshon's village street a sickly scent after the rain, the scent of the bean blossom matched anything that could be produced by a city perfumer, the elm leaves were as big as pennies, wild bees feasted on the greening willows and George Hedgecock took Lijah around the first arable crops at Ayshon. The barley came up pale green, regularly turning a darker green two weeks after coming through the warm soil. The previous tenant at Sundial had sown a little Winter wheat up Elmley Way. Yellowed after the Winter's rain and frost, by May it had stooled out, grown a dark green and was long enough to hide a hare. Lijah had planted one steep land with potatoes in April and these were peeping through the ground as May came in. George Hedgecock turned his young cattle onto the common on the 14th day of the month. Harry was now off the hill, lambing finished, and he watched his wife Esther grow fat and rosy on milk from Hedgecock's dairy, cocoa from Lady Coventry and child in her womb. Lijah's wife Jane and Esther had been busy during the dark evening making bed ticks with the other village women and knitting stockings for their menfolk.

Anne Hedgecock surprised her neighbours with the amount of butter and cheese she made. She took the hill road to Tewkesbury market on Wednesdays and got ninepence a pound for her butter. The cheese, the serving men and the family had with their bread and cider.

Lord Coventry no longer hunted the fox on Bredon Hill; the vixens were whelping in Ayshon wood, their Spring call had long ceased and now there was just the sharp bark of the dog fox as he hunted the hills for food at night.

Every morning Harry took his sheep-dog around George Hedgecock's ewes and lambs. One morning, close to a hawthorn bush in full blossom, he found a lamb frothing at the mouth with its head held back stiffly; the mother stood by bleating and stamping its forefeet at Harry's dog. The lamb was a single ewe lamb, the extended bag of the ewe showed her two teats inflamed and full of milk and Harry had no option but to kill the lamb for meat. It had swallowed wool from the thorns of the may tree with the inevitable result that the milk stayed in the gullet with the wool and curdled. Harry killed it with his knife and as soon as he had carried it down into the dairy at Sundial Farm he skinned and dressed it, taking out the pluck, or fry, and then he fetched George Hedgecock who was up with Lijah at Elmley Way cutting thistles with a jadder among his Winter wheat. George firmly believed Harry's tale, gave him the lamb's head and pluck, and together they hung the carcase to set on one of those long wooden pegs which stood out on the dairy wall.

"Shackles we got for dinner, Missus," Harry told Esther as he put the odds and ends in the iron pot with a turnip and some onions. "We'll have the liver and lights tomorrow."

"Ah," sighed Esther, "It's an ill wind that don't blow no

good. You never did, did you, Harry?" "Never done what?" Harry was puzzled as he swung the loaded pot onto the pot hook over the fire. "You never pushed that wool in that lamb's maw. It have bin done, you know, on purpose."

"If I didn't know you so well and if you hadn't got that little un under yer petticoat, dalled if I udn't put you across my knee and smack yer ass for ever suggestin' I ud do such a mean thing to a good gaffer." Esther laughed and between her laughs said, "You a carryin Lady Coventry down the hill last Winter was just an excuse for me carrying you a few nights ater on the bed tick."

May ended and the elder flowered, the potatoes grew taller, the Winter wheat burst into ear and the barley shot up straight straws between broad green leaves on George Hedgecock's farm. The first hot days of June led Harry to fold his flock of sheep and look for the fly blows and maggots. He found a few maggots on some of the long-woolled ewes' rumps and below the tail where the dung had clung to the long fleece.

"We will shear tomorrow," George Hedgecock announced as he sat with Anne in the front room of the farmhouse on the Sunday night. Anne had on a new full-length dress with a hooped skirt in blue velvet with a lace collar— George had bought it as a surprise at Stow Fair. Her eighteen-inch waist showed off her ample bust quite daringly displayed. On cold evenings she would need a 'bosom friend'. George Hedgecock's new breeches and stockings, his fitted jacket, his light Sunday shoes, his silk cravat and mutton-chop whiskers showed to the world of Ayshon just what he was— a yeoman farmer.

The Hedgecock family, sometime before this perfect June evening, had brewed a barrel of beer for the shearing and George tapped it that Sunday night as the setting sun shone through the brewhouse door. The amber liquid glistened as if sparkling to match the golden rays. Blowing the froth from his quart pot,

Harry, a good judge of beer, pronounced it good. "I just wondered," he said to Anne, "whether the water of Bredon Hill would make beer like we had on the Cotswolds." What a handsome couple they were that Sunday as they walked hand in hand from the brewhouse after Anne had agreed the beer to be palatable!

Back in the front room, all was still that evening, the light was fading, George slipped his arm around Anne's waist, drew her towards him and kissed the bloom on her peachlike cheek. Then, his heart thumping louder against his waistcoat as it pumped the blood faster through his veins until the back of his neck was a flame of fire, his tongue dry like parchment in his mouth, he took her in his strong arms and kissed her again and again on her lips as she faltered out, "Oh George, I love you, I love you, and I love the house, perhaps soon we could do what Harry and Esther did last Winter—perhaps it would be a boy to follow Mark. But dear me, George, look at the time, it's shearing tomorrow at five o'clock," and happily the couple went to bed.

The Shearing

Next morning the heavy dew foretold another hot day as Harry and his dog brought the Hedgecock flock from the hill into the empty cattle yard. While Harry penned the ewes, Lijah, Mark and George stood with their shears around the grindstone, Mark turning the handle as George ground the shear blades and tested their sharpness by chipping at bits of fallen wool, while Lijah poured water from a wooden pail over the stone. The polished elm boards of the threshing floor told the tale of age upon age of threshing and shearing. Harry had a pen of twenty ewes close to the threshing floor and with his crook he caught the first ewe by the rear left leg and walked her back onto the floor. In one moment she was sitting up like a begging dog and in another George Hedgecock had cut the first wool from around the ewe's neck and foretop. Harry and Lijah followed suit, Mark rolled up the finished fleeces as the naked, snow-white ewes ran to their lambs in the orchard.

" 'Tis thirsty work, man," Lijah called to Anne as she went into the dairy.

"You old rascal, Lijah," Anne replied. "You aren't thirsty already," but seeing the sweat dropping from his chin and the usual sweat from Harry's nose, Anne brought a large jug of the beer George Hedgecock had sampled the night before.

Work went apace as the men, after shearing several of the ewes, laxed their thirst and relaxed their nerves with the golden product of Master Barleycorn. Dinnertime was but twenty minutes this day of days, when Anne brought home baked bread, cheese and boiled bacon to keep her menfolk working happily. Two days the shearing lasted, then Harry with boiling pitch marked G.H. with a branding iron on each ewe's back, before returning the sheep to the common. Meanwhile Francis Stokes ordered Shepherd Bosley to gather Lord Waterford's flock of ewes into the paddock of Saltway barn. The hot sultry weather had caused the fly to strike a number of the ewes and Francis decided to shear immediately. The following morning he left his wife Honour and the children Andrew and Elizabeth at Cullabine Farm while he mounted his stiff cob and rode to Saltway. Shepherd Bosley had folded the ewes and his son, Norman, a strong youth of sixteen, was ready with sharpened shears to be taught how to make a tidy fleece and make a tidy job of shearing. Harry Holmes, the Squire's carter, was brought in for this urgent job. Bosley was a dab hand at shearing having been under-shepherd on another estate before coming to Ayshon. He had sheared several hundred sheep before, although the head shepherd supervised the lambing. Stripping off his smock, he stood in the barn in his cord breeches, his rough shirt and heavy leather boots with their curved shepherd's last, waiting for Norman to bring him the first ewe. After stabling his cob, Francis thought it not lowering for a bailiff to help with the shearing in an emergency. Harold Holmes sheared neither as skilfully nor quickly as Mr Stokes or Shepherd Bosley, but as Shepherd Bosley said, "Them as he shears, we shan't have to do."

Norman soon got the hang of this new work. After a few shouts from his father, "Stick yer knees into her, bwoy," the ewes no longer struggled from his grasp.

It was a picture that day in Saltway Barn. Bosley's breeches soon became stiffened by the rising grease from the wool as his boots became more supple—each ewe that he sheared added a little more grease to the leather uppers. Mr Stokes had brought some old clothes with him, making him look very different from Lord Waterford's bailiff riding his cob around the estate. Harry Holmes appeared his usual self, not hurrying over much, talking a lot except when his shears revealed a bunch of maggots and Bosley came over and rubbed them off the skin onto the threshing floor. If the skin was broken and raw from the maggots, he put a dab of Stockholm tar on the place. The Winter and Spring work on Bredon Hill had chapped Harold's hands. The grease in the wool softened them but his skin smarted when the salt from the sweating ewes went deep into the cracks.

Lord Waterford himself was at Beckford Hall and Francis, as a young bailiff, thought it wise to send his son Andrew with a message to say that shearing had begun. Lord Waterford knew his calendar pretty well and remarked to his wife, "Well, surely Stokes is shearing early this year. Maybe it's the fly." "I must encourage young Stokes," the Squire thought, so without further ado the groom was sent for and ordered to harness the horses in the nag stable—one for the Squire and one for the groom. Meanwhile wicker baskets were being prepared in the kitchen under the watchful eye of the housekeeper—cold meats and bread, gooseberry pie, costrel barrels of cider and beer. The groom had instructions to put the tandem saddle on his horse so that the prepared food could be fastened in the baskets behind the rider. The Squire rode his usual hunter. The journey from Beckford to Saltway Barn would be about three miles and a half, but the Squire was not, on this June day, following Lord Coventry's hounds heading as they so often did to Saltway Barn and the Roughts nearby, with reynard way in front, the south wind fluffing his brush and his scent difficult to follow as it blew ahead of him. No, master and man trotted quietly along the familiar wheel ruts up Rabbit Lane and through Ayshon village and onto the Saltway.

The Squire was pleased to see the shearing going so well. The men literally peeled the wool from the long coated Cotswold sheep and what fleeces! The Squire was a good judge of weights and as he felt the bound fleeces he reckoned them to be around twelve to fifteen pounds apiece. The men found the Squire's food good and wholesome as they sat down for midday bait under the shade of a chestnut tree. The shearing went well in the sun, and eating and drinking better in the shade.

This is how Lord Waterford's flock were shorn in the early summer of 1769. It took a number of days to get through the sheep (Lord Waterford had stocked the hill grazing heavily) and when it was finished the wool was stacked on hurdles in the barn. Shepherd Bosley was free to take his sheep once again on to Bredon Hill—the sheep would be free from the fly now until their fleeces grew again in the later Summer.

Harvest

The 26th of June, a Fair Day at nearby Pershore, was the official date to start mowing the meadows down by the brook for the hay. This year the 26th was a day of thunder and lightning, of rain and hail, so it was taken up with setting and sharpening scythes, putting new teeth in rakes and new sticks in shuppicks (or sheave pikes) on George Hedgecock's holding. By the 1st of July the weather improved as the wind swung round to the north, coming straight from Elmley Castle. That morning Bernard Baker sniffed the clear air as he looked at the clouds and exclaimed, "That's the sort of sandwich I likes to see—blue sky, green fields and fresh air in between. We be in for a feow days a dry weather." The whole village looked to Bernard as their weather prophet.

"Morning, Reverend," Bernard said to Phil Besford as they met in the lane. "We be gwain to have it fine I feel."

"How right you are Bernard," Phil said. "My weather glass has gone right up into fine—it's higher than it's been since the shearing."

That day men could be seen carrying their scythes towards the hay fields down by the brook. They protected their blades with hip briars—the briar of the dog rose—which acted as a sheath would to a sword. Every man's broad leather belt had a loop at the back to carry the whetstone. Like a little army they marched down Ayshon village, separating here and there as they went to their different meadow land. The ring of whetstone on scythe blade was music this July morning. "Put a long edge on yer blade and keep the knoll down," the older men told the youths, the knoll being the heel end of the blade. "Who a gwain first?"

Lijah asked Harry as he spat in his hands to get a firm grip on the scythe sned. Lijah's face seemed rosier than ever in the morning sun; Harry Steel was hanging his smock on a hawthorn with his frail basket of bait, his gallon of cider, and turning to Lijah said, ''Thee lead 'til bait time, then I'll lead after and young Mark can stay behind.''

The swish of George Hedgecock's leading men as they cut their first swathe around the field was in perfect rhythm, so even, so deliberate. As the mixture of grass and clover fell before the scythe, and as the scythe shaved so near to the ground leaving only a short stubble, slugs were exposed, snails came to light. Blackbirds and thrushes, both old and young, left their hawthorn haunts and followed the mowers to breakfast off the life exposed by the blades. On a smaller scale, the scene was that of gulls following the plough to pick up the worms disturbed from the upturned furrow.

George Hedgecock came down to the haymaking after milking and with his scythe followed behind Mark not so close as to upset a beginner but close enough to show him the rhythmic movement of man and scythe which alone makes good mowing possible. ''In time, Mark,'' he said, ''when your back stops aching and the palms of your hands get that callous of hard skin, then you'll think of the scythe as a part of your body — it comes by practice.'' Mark watched both master and man, he whet his scythe when they did and when he found a partridge sitting on her clutch of eggs, he left a clump of unmown grass around her as he had been told to do.

Two days mowing by three men and a boy knocked down perhaps five or six acres of grass. ''That's enough,'' George Hedgecock told Mark over supper of saddle of mutton, potatoes, peas from the garden, raspberries and cream.

As the family sat by the window at Sundial Farm, Catherine

and Mathilda sewed and embroidered while Mrs Hedgecock looked after the wants of her two tired and hungry men. The hay smelt sweet as honey, and underneath the swathe it remained as green as when it was cut. George Hedgecock organised his full labour force that day; all with suppicks, or hay forks, they turned the swathe, scattering the hay on the lawn of turf below. "Give it plenty of ground room," Lijah advised as Harry and he were helped by George Hedgecock, Anne, Catherine, Mathilda and a few of the village lads. Next day they raked it into windrow, straight and long across the meadow land and heel-raked it to collect every bent which the haymakers missed. "One more performance tomorrow," Lijah forecast. "What then?" Mark asked. "You'll see, thee Dad 'ull want us to put it into cocks, shaped and raked to protect it from the rain, it's amus fit to carry, it would be a pity to get it spoiled."

The hay was cocked next day—a good pitchforkful put in each cock; the overnight dew damped the tops of the cocks making them look smaller but more compact. Lijah brought two horses and a waggon down to the haymaking next morning, together with long hayforks for pitching and short ones for loading. Harry Steel brought two horses and a waggon following Lijah's. The cocks were in rows just far enough apart for the waggon to go between the avenues of hay. Mark led the foremost horse up the centre of the rows, George Hedgecock rode on the waggon and with his short shuppick he loaded the hay while Harry and Lijah pitched the cocks onto the waggon. First they filled the bed of the waggon with hay which George trampled down firmly. Then George Hedgecock shouted, "Corners on the front." Harry and Lijah didn't really need telling as they dropped a burden of hay on each corner of the raves of the waggon. "Now a pitchful between them," and Harry bound the corners with a pitchful between, right up front—'the crank

eckford Hall, Squire Lord Waterford's place.

Beckford Inn, a posting inn with seventy stables, in 1802.

BECKFORD INN 1809

Farm labourers

quad' was the expression used by farm men for the pitchful placed behind the corners. "Now corners at the back," shouted George Hedgecock, and the same routine took place as at the front. "Over," he called to the next pitcher when he wanted a pitchful under his feet. All the time there was a continuous "Hold tight" from Mark as he moved horses and waggon from cock to cock. Anne and the girls followed with their rakes so that no hay should be wasted.

When the waggons were loaded, Hedgecock's men took their teams and waggons along the road, up into the rickyard at Sundial Farm where a staddle of wood faggots lay, the hay was unloaded and George Hedgecock built his rick. As the rick grew higher, the men found it impossible to reach with their forkfuls and a pitch hole was left in the side of the rick like an intermediate platform. The hay was pitched into this hole and long-armed Harry hoisted it onto the rick.

So the routine was from Lijah on the waggon to Harry in the pitch hole and from Harry to Mark, then Mark to George Hedgecock who built the outside of the rick leaving Mark to fill in the middle. Each night the middle of the rick was left well full in case of rain, and so the hay was gathered. Francis Stokes organised Lord Waterford's men in similar fashion. Phil Besford and Abel got theirs together with the help of the young curate. Stephen Bosworth did all his work on horseback, so he got some of the smallholders to help with the haymaking.

The smallholders themselves mowed their hay on some of the village wastelands and built little ricks in their gardens and orchards for the family cow and horse. Every bent of hay in the village street was mown and gathered by these men. The labourers like Lijah, Harry, Fred Pickford, and Abel Smith had no rights on the common so worked full-time for their masters for six or seven shillings a week, with a little extra for haymaking and harvest, and they were allowed to glean after the last load of corn was in. Ayshon's haymaking was over, the crop was gathered—some weathered by the rain, but it was gathered. Then the day men, the carters and the shepherds all thatched the neat ricks with wheat straw safe against the weather.

On the last two Sundays in July, the Rev. Richard Surman took the duty at Ayshon Church. He prayed for an abundant harvest, and he went around the parish in the weeks that followed, encouraging the reapers. Jim Bradfield and Job Allen discussed the prospects of the crops in the Plough, argued how many bushels per acre the wheat and the barley would yield, then they talked of Sam Parsons's strip of wheat. "Dids't ever see such a crop?" Jim, sticking out his bristly chin, challenged the company. "Well I'll be dalled," Bernard Baker spoke. "Unt it to be expected? Didn't ya see Sam working late las' September hauling his pig muck and the cleaning from his petty out into his strip? He borrowed Phil Besford's hoss and cart. Then he plastered it with wood ash and ploughed it and he's a gwain to git a rip-roaring crop." "Good luck to him, I says, he got a wife and little uns to keep," Job Allen belched as the acid from the cider caught his breath.

"How many family 'as the Bailey brought with him?" Job ventured this question to the regulars in the tap room of the Plough.

"Oi, that's a ussy un," Jim countered. "Thur's Francis Stokes, his wife Honour, Andrew and Elizabeth."

"Thee bist one short and it a bin kept quiet, Honour had another son this morning. Lady Waterford went to Cullabine in the two 'oss chaise and put a new George the Third guinea in the little un's hand at dinner time. Honour brought that un under her petticoat when her come yur."

After the little group had gone to their homes as the Summer sun set behind the fir trees above Beckford, Charlie Baker, the parish clerk, was taken ill with a sudden inflammation of the stomach. As the night went on, the Archdeacon's doctor rode over from Tewkesbury but could do little except apply hot poultices of linseed with doses of laudanum to ease the pain. Charles died on the first day of August. That first day of harvest, Charles, who had dug so many graves in Ayshon churchyard clay, now returned to clay. His wife, Olive and the bachelor son, Jack, wept as Charles lay rigid on the sofa awaiting the elm coffin wheelwright Miles shaped the next day. Jack was a bastard son of Olive's but Charles, his father, had made him respectable, giving him his name when he married Olive the following year. Archdeacon Trusswell and the Rev. Richard Surman conducted the funeral service in St Andrew's church at Ayshon. The parish clerk's coffin was carried shoulder high up the churchyard after travelling on the wooden bier from his cottage. The carriers were his friends at the Plough Inn— Jim Bradfield, Job Allen, Sam Parsons and Fred Pitchford—and the gravedigger from Elmley Castle acted as sexton that day.

Charles's son, Jack, was to succeed his father as clerk and sexton later. The robed choir sang in memory of the old clerk. The orchestra in the gallery provided the music; one thing was missing— the deep rich notes of Charles Baker's own bass viol. It lay silent, propped up in the corner of the musicians' gallery, and everyone hoped that Jack would follow his father in yet another way and play the bass viol at church. Jack wore his black suit and a black hat band, and the whole company of villagers wore black gloves as a mark of respect to Clerk Baker.

" 'Twas Father's wish to be buried anant the old yew tree," Jack had told the Elmley sexton. As the fine Ayshon soil was sprinkled on the coffin, the villagers viewed the box containing the mortal remains of their old clerk, then they read on the brass plate: 'Charles Baker died August 1st 1769 aged 62.' Back at the house the Rev. Richard Surman, the bearers and family mourners consoled Olive Baker and Jack over a feast of veal, beans and ham, a piece of boiled beef and gooseberry pie helped down with rhubarb wine Charles had made in the Spring. Richard Surman then hurried back to church Honour Stokes who had so recently given birth to a son. The villagers felt relieved that this was being done and Francis Stokes gave the curate a guinea for his trouble. Why were the people of Ayshon so relieved? It was common knowledge that had Honour gone into any other house except the House of God before she had been duly churched, there would have been a birth in that house within twelve months. Stephen Bostock, who had been to the funeral, a ratepayer of the parish, put it like this: "We have too many bastards to keep now out of the parish funds—take Meg Dance, the farmer Edward Dance's daughter, she's got four and boasts that if she had one more bastard she could live comfortable off the rates, better than being married."

"Meg's like the front door lock, anybody can put the key in as a got one," Jim Bradfield said. "'Tis like it with some women," added Job Allen, still at the rhubarb wine, "when they wants it, they a got to have it."

But the church, the parson, the clerk and the churching of women had to be forgotten for the next six weeks, excepting of course on Sundays. The corn was ripe and ready to cut. The Squire's men under Francis Stokes started first on the wheat with their bagging hooks and pitchthanks (the wooden hook used to bring out the sheaf). The sound of whetstone on blade could be heard on the still dewy mornings of early August. The men worked around the fields of corn, round and round the same way as the clock—without taking notice of the clock. They worked to bring out their sheaves from dawn until dusk. Their womenfolk followed, tying the sheaves with straw bands, using the same knot that their grandmothers had used.

The smallholders took off what days they were allowed by their masters to harvest their strips of wheat and later barley. Oftentimes the women cut this with their saw-edged sickles, grasping a handful of ears in the left hand and using the sickle with a sawing action. They laid the straw and ears on their straw bands until the sheaf was big enough to tie. But the main harvest was cut by hook and by crook, for the sickles left long stubble.

George Hedgecock had mainly barley this harvest. Arriving the previous Michaelmas gave him little time to prepare for Winter wheat, although the previous tenant had planted one small piece. Anyway George Hedgecock was no novice at barley growing and harvesting. Didn't he have the patience when farming on the Cotswold to wait for the seed to come up? Didn't his father use the phrase many times when things grew slowly on that bleak upland, "It's as slow coming up as Cotswold barley"?

With scythes still gleaming from haymaking, George Hedgecock, Harry, Lijah and Tom Steel, now thirteen, mowed the barley in swathes, leaving little stubble. The Summer sun made both standing and cut corn crackle in the heat and changed the look and colour of Ayshon and Bredon Hill landscape. The golden ears of wheat changed almost to red as they stood in their stooks and when the barley was cut it left a more uniform cream stubble lined with the swathes of barley.

The farmers and smallholders were fortified by bread, cheese and fat bacon baits at midday under the shade of Ayshon's oaks and elms, their thirsts slaked by last year's cider. After a few dry days the barley was moved out of the swathes on the stubble by shuppicks into wads. The wads were built like haycocks but smaller, almost small enough to pitch at one forkful into the waggons. The few oats grown for the hunting horses were cut and stooked and were supposed to wait out in the fields until the farmer had been to church three times before they were carried in the waggons and ricked.

The more experienced men of the village placed mushroom-shaped staddlestones in position in the village rickyard near the threshing barns, then fixed large timbers from stone to stone, crossing these with smaller timber then faggots of brushwood tied in bundles by withies, so forming a foundation for the wheat ricks. As Lord Waterford's men and his horses and oxen brought home the harvest, the rick builders built their ricks of sheaves, the ears all facing the middle of the rick, the butt end of the sheaves to the outside. The waggons were loaded in the same fashion. The ricks varied like the parish churches; some builders preferred the square shape of the church tower, some the round spire of other churches. The roof of the square or rectangular rick was finished like that of a house, while the spire was finished with one sheaf at the top as the builder drew in the roof course by course. It was a tidy job.

The barley was quite another story. The barley mow usually went in the barn; Francis Stokes used all the barn space he had to stack his barley. Unlike the wheat, it didn't settle with the night dews and so as fast as the waggons brought in the loads he got Harold Holmes to bring one of his quieter horses to press it down. As the loads of barley came in, up and up went the stack and up and up went Harold and the old horse. "How be us gwain to get him down?" Shepherd Bosley questioned. "Thee 'ull see in a feow minutes," Harold said. With the horse and man high on the stack, he tied a plough rein on the old horse who had done the job before, and said quietly, "Keep Dobbin". He pulled the rein and they both slid off the barley mow.

"Harold got a way with 'osses," young Norman Bosley said as the carter took Dobbin back to the stable.

The Rev. Phil Besford of Highford House and Abel his plough-man harvested their small acreage with the aid of Richard Surman, the curate, and a few volunteers. "His cider is as good as any I've tasted," Bernard Baker told his friends at the Plough after a day working with two men of the cloth.

And so at last the harvest was in. The little strips of arable the commoners held dear had been shorn of their corn, and the corn built into tidy ricks near the village building ready for the Winter's threshing. They were thatched and tidy to keep out the rain. The big ricks of Lord Waterford and Stephen Bostock and George Hedgecock's wheat rick gave the parish an air of pros-perity. The harvest of corn and fruit, the harvest of garden vegetables was such that no one starved, though many could have done with a greater variety of food.

The Hon. John Franklin, young and gallus, saw his father's barns filled with plenty but did little at Beckford to help with the in-gathering. He coursed his dogs for hares these September mornings with great success and, with Burman the groom, pro-vided many a brace off Bredon Hill for the Hall table. He rode to Worcester for the cock fights, he gambled heavily, but again with great success, and on September 12th he won fifty golden guineas at the cockfighting, arriving back at midnight at Beckford Hall the worse for drink.

That same day, Caleb Mason, an invalid late shepherd to Lord Waterford, died alone in his cottage on Bredon Hill. He was the last of a long line of shepherds who knew every nook and cranny of the hill. His childless wife had died some five years previously. Phil Besford, one time parson, now a gentleman farmer, visited him and was good to him. Phil was still a clerk in Holy Orders and Caleb had so often asked him to bury him when the time came. The Archdeacon agreed, so three days after, Caleb, the hill shepherd, was laid in Ayshon's churchyard to await the call of the Great Shepherd.

"I never went to church very often, seldom did I take the wine and wafer," he confessed to Phil. "How does I stand when I meets me Maker?" Phil explained to him the need he had met by his shepherding on the hill, how God understood, but Caleb got him to promise to tuck a good handful of sheep's wool under his chin so that Saint Peter, when he met him at the gate of heaven, would understand his poor attendance. Phil also saw to it that Ayshon's carpenter and coffin-maker put Caleb's smock and crook in the box. No feasting and drinking after Caleb's funeral; no relatives left, but just enough money to pay Carpenter Brown for his work—nine shillings, in fact—and to pay the bearers. Phil did the duty at the church out of kindness. The bearers and young Jack Baker, the new sexton who said the Amens very well for the first time, then went up to Highford House as guests to a meal with the Rev. Phil Besford and his housekeeper Mary Barnes. So Caleb, the last of the Mason family to tend the Bredon Hill sheep, was laid at the very foot of Bredon Hill. The harvest was over, Caleb had been gathered in with the corn of 1769.

Coronation Day Celebrations

September 22nd marked the day eight years before when King George III was crowned our king. Lord Waterford and Arch- deacon Trusswell thought it fitting that in rural parishes like Beckford and Ayshon this should be celebrated as a day of feast- ing and rejoicing. George III had associated with forward-looking agriculturists like Jethro Tull, Lord Townshend, Bakewell, and

"Farmer George" during his reign developed the model farm at Windsor.

Great rejoicings both at Beckford and Ayshon were the order of the day. Bells rang all day long from the two towers, cudgel playing was indulged in by the youths of both parishes and rustic sports on Bredon Hill. The ancient sports of shin-kicking, bare-fisted boxing for belts and Morris dancing were all held, and the whole countryside ran riot for just one day. The horses had a feeling of Sunday as lazily they lay in the home paddocks of both manors. True, one team with a waggon took the food and drink nine hundred odd feet up Bredon Hill to that great outcrop of rock known as the Bambury Stone. Here, at the expense of the Squire and Parson, a huge bonfire was erected right on top of the hill overlooking the River Avon. Here the rustic sports took place. The fireworks, which came from London, were let off by Bailey Stokes after dark—sky rockets, mines, tree crackers, wheels and various Indian fireworks.

Near the Bambury Stone, villagers from the two villages flocked in their hundreds. At midday, as the sun turned the damp dewy grass into slippery wire, the races were run. The half mile heat for women was won by Catherine Hedgecock; she did it in three minutes and was pleased with her prize of a set of shift ribbons. The beer from Lord Waterford's brewhouse, tapped from the wood, had varying effects on the labourers, the cottage farmers, the stockmen and the farmers of the hill villages. Lijah Hicks sang to the music of the Ayshon church orchestra. His deep voice echoed from Fiddlers Knap, the clump of beeches near the Bambury Stone, to the stone barn at Sheldons. The revellers joined in his songs as each chorus came round. Jack Baker played the bass viol almost as well as his father. "Charlie Baker won't be dead as long as Jack's alive," Jim Bradfield shouted when the music stopped.

The singing and the dancing went on through the day, the servant girls and ploughboys taking round the food and drink as, like an army resting between the battle, villagers rested on the grassy banks with bread and boiled beef, mugs of cider and beer, pieces of roasted rabbit soused with onions, apple pies and all the other good things. The King was being remembered with his Queen Charlotte. No one knew then that she would bear him fifteen children.

As the sun was low in the sky over the Malverns and the shadows of men, women and little children lengthened, as men were merry with ale and cider and women and children had their full of furmity, Mathilda Hedgecock slipped away towards the parish quarry. Archdeacon Trusswell's nephew, a young man of nineteen on leave from the Military Academy, went with her—a prearranged diversion, no doubt. Gregory Trusswell, a well spoken young man, smart in his military uniform, was more than attracted by Mathilda's raven black hair, hair which she could sit on when she rested on the fireside settle. Mathilda's cream and roses complexion was the reward of healthy fare at Sundial's table and the healthy air of Bredon Hill. Young Gregory was the only child of his widowed mother. His father had been killed in battle in one of the off-and-on wars which had become a habit between Britain and France.

The rabbits scuttled to their holes as Gregory and Mathilda walked hand in hand down the stepping stones hewn out of the limestone rock by generations of parishioners who had made use of the quarry. At the bottom of the workings, where the passing of time had allowed the cornflowers, the hardheads and the wild thyme to form a thick luxurious carpet, Mathilda and Gregory sat holding hands, saying nothing while the rabbits dared to come out again from their holes. The sheep on Bredon Hill wandered for miles over unenclosed common, Hedgecock's sheep, Waterford's sheep, Bostock's sheep. As the first evening stars shone bright over Cotswold Edge, the flocks of woolly Cotswold ewes followed their distinct runs through the grassy banks of Ayshon's quarry. Last Spring's lambs were grazing the common arable strips, clearing up the harvest stubble in the vale. The ewes would not have long to wait before what was known as the riding season. The tups or rams would be turned out on St Luke's Day, 18th October— 'At St Luke's Day, let tup have play'.

From where Gregory and Mathilda sat on the edge of the quarry bottom, they could see and hear everything as daylight turned to twilight. The rabbits became bolder, the sheep lay still in the shelter of the quarry, a covey of partridges nestled down for the night in a waggon wheel track, the metallic clink, clink, clank of the cock birds stirring the bold rabbits. Gregory told of the life at the Academy. He spoke of drill with flintlock guns, parades and bands. Mathilda, the Cotswold country dairy-maid, was enraptured by the manly talk and his manly bearing. "Let me dream on if I am dreaming," she thought as she fingered lightly the buttons on his tunic. She smoothed his thick golden hair as he lay hatless half reclining on the grass. Gregory, who had had many adventures with city girls in their finery, felt different on Bredon Hill with George Hedgecock's daughter. As they lay together on the grass, the rockets at the Bambury stone shot skywards, descending like shooting stars. The lovers cared little about rockets and bonfires as they watched the throng of villagers dancing in the distance around the fire. As Gregory tenderly held Mathilda's ample bosom and stole a kiss, she flung her arms around his military collar and clung to him as the Doctor's leech clung sucking a patient's blood. As they rolled over on dew-drenched grass she lay in his arms like a child. She had been a child until this night.

"What are you thinking of, Greg?" she ventured.

"I don't know whether I should tell you, but first— can I call you Tilda?"

" 'Course you can, but what's on your mind?"

Greg pulled her even closer to him, her raven black hair fell across his chest and the twinkle in her eyes was matched only by the twinkle of the stars over Cotswold Edge. The moon rose over Pinnock Wood and the Academy, arms drill and parades were far from his thoughts.

"I was thinking," he said, "of St Luke's Day. Each tup will have forty or so ewes to mate with."

"What's that to do with us?" Tilda answered, half knowing his thoughts.

"A beautiful black-haired girl with rosy cheeks, warm soft bosoms, a carefree smile— a farmer's daughter I had in mind. I've often heard Uncle preach about choirs of angels and I've heard them tonight, Tilda."

"But we musn't, Greg. What would Father say if you got me in the family way, and you abroad, perhaps with your regiment when you've finished your training?"

"No, I'm not going abroad yet," Greg explained. When he had his commission he would be at Tydlesley barracks with his regiment. "Will you marry me then, about next June? You'll be eighteen and I'll be twenty."

"Oh Greg," Tilda flung herself completely on his broad chest, "Oh Greg, I'm so happy, of course I'll marry you. Mother and Father will be pleased, I'm sure." They fell asleep, Tilda folded in his arms with his great coat wrapped around them both. They woke to the sound of Jack Baker and his little group of fiddlers accompanying him and the throng of villagers singing "Britons never shall be slaves".

The sheep suddenly stirred, a drunken man swayed right on the edge of an outcrop of stone above the quarry, his silhouette standing out boldly in the moonlight. He was fat with a round face, his waistcoat was bursting at the buttons. Greg ran to the foot of the rock face and recognised Lijah Hicks, George Hedgecock's waggoner. " 'Tis you is it, Mathilda.'' His voice slurred through his missing front teeth, his face rosy red, his corded legs unsteady. "Don't venture that way, Lijah,'' Greg shouted, "I'm coming to give you a hand.'' Tilda followed up the sheep track and between them they guided Lijah back onto the footpath to Ayshon.

"Bist a gwain Ayshon road, you two lovebirds? If so I'll come along with ya.'' Lijah's request could not easily be refused. All the revellers had left Bredon Hill, and Lijah might fall as he nearly had done into the quarry. Once on the footpath Lijah kept steadily on for Ayshon. Greg and Tilda followed just far enough behind to keep an eye on him, just far enough behind for Greg to steal the odd kiss as his warm winter coat wrapped them as one, with his arm tight around Tilda's waist. After two miles, as the plain gave way to the steeper banks, Lijah fell on the rough grass among the gorse, not hurting himself in the least. He sat down inviting the lovers to join him. "It's bin a remarkable day on the hill,'' he said. "I beat the Ayshon and Beckford men at shin kicking,'' he added showing the couple the marks of the kicks under his gaiters. "I a won the belt, yer it is around the top of me breeches.'' Sure enough, Lijah had won the belt given by the Squire for the best man at this vicious sport. "You a bin sweethearting I gather. Don't think I be prying into your affairs.'' "Not at all,'' Greg answered, at the same time noticing that his fall had sobered Lijah up.

"I minds the time when I sweethearted Jane up at Cosgrove, it don't seem long ago now. Does you want any advice for what it's worth from an old hand?'' Tilda giggled out, "Yes, go on.'' "Never do the last job fust.'' "What on earth does he mean?''

Greg said to Tilda in a low voice so that the waggoner could not hear. "Remember St Luke's Day and what you said about the tups," replied Tilda. Lijah rambled on about when he courted Jane night after night on the barley straw in a Cotswold barn. "Bundling, they did call it and her wore bundling stockings. Then we bundled in bed and very soon there was a little un on the way. Parson told me off, charged me for the wedding and all. He never charged them as was supposed to be respectable labourers. 'Tis a bad start for young folk afore they got time to get the nest ready." As the couple said goodnight to Lijah at one o'clock in the morning outside his cottage at Sundial Farm, George Hedgecock, horn lantern in hand, came out of the barn where he had been helping a farrowing sow. "It's you, is it Greg? Out with my daughter. I hopes you've had a good time. I knew Tilda was in good company but you better get on that cob of yours and get back to the vicarage at Beckford. Come into the brewhouse first and taste my beer and you, Tilda, take a glass of port off the dresser and off to bed. Your Mother's butter-making tomorrow."

With a merry heart Greg rode the two miles to Beckford. Tilda dreamt of smart army officers and all night long felt Greg's arms around her. "Don't do the last job first," echoed the slurred voice of Lijah. No, but next June I'll walk down the aisle of Saint Andrew's an officer's wife. Tilda had experienced love for the first time.

CHAPTER THREE
New Lives

John Wesley. In 1764 he preached at Ayshon Cross on
his way to the Midlands.

Designed & Engraved by F. Eginton, Birm.^m

And another good Lady of delicate taste.
Cries "Fye. Mr Bookseller, bring me some paste.
I'll close up this leaf, or my daughter will skim.
The cream of that vile methodistical hymn.

Published 1807

Fear of Methodism!

BEFORE THE PRESENCE of Dissenters from the Established Church was familiar in the two villages, Quakers who lived at Beckford were making hosiery in Tewkesbury—shirts at 3s 9d each, women's shifts 4s 6d, Linsey petticoats 4s 7d, stockings 1s 8d, bed gowns 5s 6d, linen sheets 13s, hurden sheets 1s 6d, leather breeches 8s, and so on. Presbyterians had come and gone at Ayshon as conditions changed.

Then in 1764 John Wesley visited Tewkesbury on 9th May. Coming through Gutherton he preached at Ayshon cross on his way to the Midlands. The older strip holders, the cottage farmers, the squatters on the common, all flocked to hear the great man, the man who had not come to preach dissent but was forming societies up and down the country, the Tewkesbury one being particularly strong. As he travelled the country, he made friends with several parsons of the Established Church, courting two daughters of a local vicar.

"Love Feasts, they be holding at Tewkesbury," Abel Smith told Fred Pickford as he propped his tired feet on the pig bench as the two sat together by the Plough fire.

"Thee bist got too old for that caper, Abel. 'Tis nourishment thee dost want, not punishment."

Abel, who often went on Wednesdays to the market, said: "It unt what you imagine; 'tis a sort of common Holy Communion."

"Only the Archdeacon and Surman can minister that," Fred replied. "And thee knowst it."

Abel had found out that for the most part the Tewkesbury Methodists had communion in the Abbey in the morning and then met, as a society and not a sect, in the evening and broke the bread at a Love Feast. "I a bin to these yer Love Feasts," Abel admitted, "and they beunt dissenters. It's a society as meets at night and in the wick."

"Old Trusswell won't welcome this lot in Ayshon and thee hads't better look out, Abel, working for Phil Besford and living in one of his houses."

Abel said, "I'd a mind to join em. The church be got corrupt and the rich be treated different to the poor."

As the lovers of Perkins's homebrewed beer, brewed in his own brew house, said their farewells that night, one man was worried—Jack Baker, the Parish Clerk. It wasn't that he had any worries about his job under Trusswell and Surman but he didn't want a Society of Methodists in Ayshon. "They will bring discontent," he thought. Up till now, Richard Surman kept a morning school for the children of gentlefolk—the farmers and suchlike. If Wesley came often he would start weeknight class meetings. Men who had so far only learnt pieces from the prayer-book by heart—uneducated men, labourers, copy holders and such—would learn to read the Bible, possibly to write.

Wesley came again to Tewkesbury and once was diverted through Ayshon on his way to Worcester. Bengeworth—an outpost of A'sum—had a vicar sympathetic to Methodism; after all didn't Beale and Cooper become his friends? Wesley soon had a following and a society was formed under Abel Smith. Ten members joined meeting at Ayshon Wood House, the home of Jonah Stubbs who had a small enclosed holding there of which he owned the freehold, bought from Waterford some years back. John Wesley addressed the first meeting, imploring the society to take communion at St Andrew's. He told them they had a good man in the Rev. Richard Surman, but could not say the same about Archdeacon Trusswell of Beckford.

"What about Love Feasts?" Abel asked.

"They will be administered by my man from Tewkesbury—but not often. You must meet on Wednesdays over the word of God and I'm sure that Jonah Stubbs will lead you in the right paths."

Archdeacon Trusswell, who held Ayshon's living, was furious at the intrusion. He thought it fitting to consult Lord Waterford on the situation. They decided that in future no follower of Wesley should be allowed a house if one became vacant. The retired vicar, Phil Besford, looked after by Mary Barnes as his housekeeper at Higford House and farming his small farm with Abel Smith, considered this new phase in Ayshon's history thoughtfully.

"Abel," he said, calling in at the stable one October morning in 1769, "I've heard you have joined the Methodist Society and meet in the wood. I'm glad you have taken an interest in the scriptures, but don't become an agitator or a dissenter. I've spoken to Richard Surman and he will allow you communion at St Andrew's."

"I a sin the light like Paul did a-gwain to Damascus. Wesley says I be well on the road to heaven. Surman's all right but I a got a score to settle along uv the Archdeacon."

The next Saturday afternoon the Archdeacon's coach came up Beckford Road. Trusswell called the coachman to a halt as Abel strolled along the lane out of the village.

"What's this I hear that you and Jonah Stubbs have started in Ayshon Wood? Are you denying the power of the bishops? Are you not rising above your station? You are but a labourer, you don't even have a strip of arable, nor grazing rights. Besford could throw you out of house and home for this."

"Wesley told us when he come," Abel answered, "that we beunt a breaking away from the church but just forming a society for the betterment of our souls and minds."

"To hell with Wesley," retorted Trusswell. "I'll have him put in the River Avon."

"The first time that I knowed you was in favour of adult baptism, Master Trusswell."

"What did he tell my people on the village cross? Out with it man."

"He told us that there was one mediator between God and man and that was not the Bishops, but Christ. He also told us to repent, which I have done."

"Anything else, Smith?" the Archdeacon snorted as Burman the groom and coachman had some difficulty holding his horses.

"Yes, that we was all equal in the sight of God. Naked we comes into the world and naked we goes out."

"Haven't I preached that very thing at St Andrew's, you'll bear me out with that, Burman?"

"Yes, sir," Burman said.

"Oi, we be about as equal as the rich man and Lazarus in the Bible. Stubbs read that out Sunday night."

"What do you mean, Smith? I'm in a hurry but I'll listen."

Abel Smith had never spoken man to man with the Archdeacon before; besides, the reverend gentleman also being chairman of the court, Abel felt he could be flung in jail. " 'Tis like this, sir. You talks of equality in the sight of God, now I be more or less satisfied with my work, Master Besford is very good to me, but when we come to church Sunday morning it be different. You takes the elements first at Communion, which is right, but what happens after? Fust it's Lord and Lady Waterford and Sir John Franklin in their warm pews by the stove, velvet cushions they sits on. Then comes the farmers, the wheelwrights, the baker, the cottage farmers and the strip holders with their grazing rights—they sits amust at the back on them hard cold pews. Then we feow labourers, 'tis pitiful to see us, amus too

ashamed to darken the door of God's house. Thur we sits on the
bench by the door in our smock frocks and blackleaded hobnail
boots, our heads bowed. Anant us sits the shepherds, their dogs
chained to the pew ends when they be able to come. You a sin
the pew end anant the door with the knobs on um amus worn
away by the dog chains. We be perished. When we walks up to
the holy table, we be so ashamed our yuds be bowed, no one
spakes to us. Be us equal or no in God's sight? We be around the
table at Stubbs in Ayshon Wood house." Abel finished with these
words: " 'Tis hard for a rich man to enter the Kingdom of
God." Trusswell took the whip from the coachman and with his
horses at the canter he left Abel Smith in the middle of the road.

Proctor Perkins, the Plough's landlord, invited Abel and
Jonah down to the inn on the Monday to tell the company
exactly what was going on up in Ayshon Wood and what Abel
had told the Archdeacon. Fred Pickford was primed with
Perkins's home brewed ale and was talkative and argumentative.
"You chaps be making a rod for your own back. You'll suffer
and your families," Fred began. "What light ast thee sin, Abel,
apart from when you fust saw daylight?"

"I a bin born agun, Fred. Born a the spirit," replied Abel.

"I udn't go up into that 'ood uv a night if I was thee, thee bist
seeing things, Abel."

Jonah Stubbs then told the company Wesley had convinced
him there was a mansion in the skies for him when he left Ayshon
village.

"Now I be a gwain to tell you chaps summat as perhaps you
don't know" (Fred had a lot to say this night). "I a bin talkin'
to young Gregory Trusswell when he was yur on furlough.
That's the Archdeacon's nevvy, he a bin to Southampton.
Ayshon Wood rings out some nights when you Methodys sings
your hymns. Greg heard you the other night singing 'Thur is a

land of pure delight where saints immortal reign, Infinite day excludes the night and pleasures banish pain'. Isaac Watts wrote that at Lymington near Southampton where Gregory a bin; he was on the beach thur by the sea, so they say, a looking over at the Isle of Wight. I'll wager Jonah nor Abel ull think about that when the clay sticks to the plough come Winter.''

The Society stood firm regardless. Neither Besford nor Richard Surman interfered. Fred Pickford, who worked for Master Bostock, didn't join the Methodists. He not only frequented the Plough at Ayshon but went further afield to the Mill at Elmley Castle within Lord Coventry's estate. He talked with woodmen, gamekeepers, cottage farmers and the like, all of them loyal to the Established Church of St Matthew. The villagers of Elmley had heard of Abel and Jonah forming a society of Methodists at Ayshon, and, supping their pots of ale, cautioned Fred of the possible consequences.

''Yur's a case,'' one of the Elmley men told him. ''A family in the parish here be Quakers, a farming family, and I'll go to hell if the parson from Bredon don't seize some of their crops year in year out—priest's dues, they call it. Jonah Stubbs as farms that little farm in Ayshon Wood, the Archdeacon ull be after some of his crops if he don't support the church. Jack Baker, the clerk, ull be under orders from Trusswell.''

Fred, back in Ayshon, warned the villagers. Jack Baker, besides being clerk, held the office of poundsman. The village pound at Ayshon was a walled enclosure of about half an acre just below Hedgecock's farm, the whole area being shaded by chestnut trees. Archdeacon Trusswell was a rich man and he decided not to press the point of Stubbs not fully supporting the church, but he did order the poundsman not to be lenient with any member of the Methodist Society whose cattle broke out from the common or the arble fields out of season and damaged the crops. Jack, helped at times by the overseer or village constable, drove cattle, sheep, pigs, and horses from growing crops and enclosed them in the pound. He was entitled to sums of money from the owner before they could be reclaimed. What he charged was agreed by the Vestry meeting but Trusswell could, and did, make exceptions. Besides this, all farmers, tenant farmers and cottage farmers, in fact all who kept livestock, paid Jack Baker a fixed due every Christmas for his work as pounds-man. Fred Pickford meant well when he spoke of his experiences to the Ayshon folk. He walked a great deal around the villages and to the town of A'sum. He didn't hold with the A'sum Quakers refusing to take the oath in court, nor did he approve of their attending court with their hats on, as they had done in his grandfather's time.

"I be no scholar, but I believes in Church and State," he pronounced in Proctor Perkins's beer house one Saturday night. "The next pot I'll drink to Farmer George the Third. Rev. Surman told us only last Sunday from St Andrew's pulpit of troubles in France and America. Dall it," he went on to say, "if only I'd got arable strips and common rights on Bredon Hill, I'd be a happy man. I'll tell ya, Emma's got a job to make them feow shillings a wick go round. I'm only a labourer for Master Bostock. I as to laugh though, mind, when Jack Baker buries a dissenter or a suicide or an unchristened babby in the North side of the churchyard. Ayshon's clay and Beckford's gravel unt no colder thur than t'other side."

From Thatched Cottage to Stately Home

As the November fogs came down on Ayshon's street in 1769, Esther Steel grew so big of belly and bosom with her unborn child that only with slackened stays, gored and gussetted skirts could she have a reasonable amount of comfort in dress. As she and Harry lay these autumn nights under the thatch after Harry had helped her up the steep narrow stairs which he called the wooden hill, her time grew near.

Harry smiled away those November nights when the unborn child gave an extra kick against his night shirt. "I can't help thinking," he said, "the number a times I a felt a calf, weeks afore he av sin the light of day, kick against my brow when I bin milking the incalf mother."

"Now don't thee start comparing me with animals, Harry," Esther replied.

"Thee hast bin through this performance afore, not like Lady Coventry," Harry reminded her.

"What about Lady Coventry?" Esther snapped.

"Well," Harry went on, "urs fine in the bone, it's ur fust but ur won't be better until urs worse. I've been thinking of some of the capers I've had with the yearling yows when they has thur fust lamb. Some of the poorer ones had little milk on Bredon Hill."

"If you persists in talking like that, Harry, what sort of milker ull I be?" Esther was a bit annoyed with her husband's earthiness.

"Your two great tits hangs heavy, Esther. I'll warrant thur's plenty a milk for two youngsters."

"Oi, and Lady Coventry ud hang heavy on thee now, Harry. I'd give anything to see you carry her down Bredon Hill again."

Next morning Lord Coventry's groom rode over from Croome Court with a message that her Ladyship's time was nearly up and she expected a happy event any day.

"They be allus anxious with the fust," said Harry. "I suppose that means the two hoss chaise is coming to fetch Esther and little Lucy. That leaves me to cope with Tom." The chaise came later, and Harry helped Esther to pack the things she would want. "Thee bisn't a gwain short at the Court, Esther. Still, we be doing a good turn and they be doing us one."

Harry stood under his walnut tree by the front door wiping his dripping nose; the crowsfeet under his eyes gave his swarthy face a look of devilment, almost completely closing his dark brown eyes and making his hairy brows above bushier than ever.

"What's thur to laugh about?" Esther turned to him. "Be you glad to see the back of me for a bit?"

"No," Harry said. "But I was talking to Abel last night and he had been reading his Bible agun about Moses in the rushes. If we has a bwoy, call him Moses cause he is a gwain to be reared like he was in a palace."

As the farewells were said, young Tom cried and Harry again wiped his nose and a tear from the corner of his eye.

At Croome Court, Esther's room was ready—a nursery in fact. Lucy joined her brother, page boy David, and stayed in the kitchen with the maids. Lord Coventry had been to the opening meet of the fox hounds, a local run by Avon's river. Lady Coventry, who sat reading by the drawing-room fire, sent a servant girl for Esther to leave the nursery and join her for a cup of tea. "Delighted to see you again, Esther," she said. "You are looking well, I hope you have taken care."

Esther sat back on the sofa and sipped her tea and talked very quietly. She explained that she had had three children, "and Harry says that I have them like shelling peas, but it's not quite like that. I've done my work until lately except that I haven't hung out the washing, Harry's done that. I've took raspberry leaf tea like you have lately and am most grateful to come to your house and be waited on and visited by a doctor, a most unusual thing."

"Doctor Saunders has been here several times," Lady

Coventry said, "and his opinion is that everything is going on all right. He says it will be a boy—something to do with the way I carry it."

Esther laughed as she said, "I do hope we bwoth have bwoys. I hope you will excuse Harry's humour but he declares I shall have one. He kept his stockings on a purpose the night he got about me." This remark sent her Ladyship into hoots of laughter as the two reclined by the fireside. "That's a new one, Esther, keeping his stockings on."

"Harry's like that, bless his soul," said Esther.

Next morning, Doctor Saunders rode over from Worcester and examined the two mothers-to-be. "Don't know as I likes a man examining my parts," Esther told one of the maids. "It's allus bin the midwife afore."

The following few days dragged on with the odd visit from the parson and lots of attention from the maids. Two o'clock in the morning of the 5th November, Lady Coventry's pains started. Doctor Saunders rode through the morning hours from Worcester. When he arrived she was normal again but they started within the hour. He took his Lordship aside into the study and explained it might take a little time, being the first one, but he would remain until it was over. A woman used to these cases stayed with him. By five o'clock Esther Steel cried from her bedroom. Dr Saunders and the woman helper went up and found Esther had broken the water and was well on the way to childbirth. As the multitude of clocks at Croome Court struck six, Esther gave birth to a boy—Moses was born and would spend his infancy in a mansion. Lady Coventry continued in labour all the morning giving birth to her firstborn boy at noon. Could anything have ended more happily? Both babies on the fifth of November, both boys.

Straightway Lord Coventry ordered the bells of Earls Broughton to ring all day. His hunting friends joined him at Croome Court for celebrations that night. The wine ran freely and the fireworks were let off — not just because it was Guy Fawkes day but because two families were happy, each with the birth of a son.

The groom rode to Ayshon to tell Harry and all Harry could say was, "Another Moses, I'll be dalled."

Esther played her part well. She fed and cuddled the two babies with an inbred mother's love. Lady Coventry was slightly envious of Esther's way with babies but she did have to consider his Lordship and the social life at Croome Court and in London.

Back at Ayshon, Harry Steel had started winter foddering Hedgecock's cows. Every day he climbed Bredon Hill where the tups were busy on the Cotswold ewes, and once again the cycle turned as Autumn gave way to early Winter frosts and back came the fieldfares to the fruits and berries. George Hedgecock took Lijah Hicks and young Tom Steel from the plough to help him and Harry with the cider-making. The heavy gelding, Diamond, was hitched to the cider mill, walking in circles around the stone trough, pushing with his broad chest tight against the collar. The huge round stone, as it circulated the stone trough, crushed the apples to a brown pomace. It crushed the very pips in the apples until George gave the order for both pulp and new cider to be carried by Lijah and Harry and tipped into the press from which the amber liquid flowed to the waiting tubs. Tom fed Diamond on sweet hay as he stood nervously in the strange half-dark of the thatch roofed cider mill. When the last drop of cider had flowed from the press, the pomace was taken out like a huge cheese and fed to the cattle or, when dry, burned on the kitchen fire.

"This ull be a drop of good, Master Hedgecock," Lijah said as he tried a tot straight from the press.

"Can I taste some Dad?" Tom asked Harry.

"Just one tot, no more or else you ull be up the garden in the privvy all night."

The cider was turned from tub to the barrels and soon fermented, discharging the scum, the odd leaf and so on through the bung hole, until such time as men who were born for such work decided to bung it down and leave it to mellow.

Brewing the beer was not so seasonal. George Hedgecock kept his best barley in stock and brewed when levels of his barrels were low. The wet grains of one particular brew, when most of the malt had been extracted, were shovelled into a heap near the pig pens. "A few buckets of that will do the in-farrow sows good," George Hedgecock told Harry. Now Harry was a man who liked his animals to have as many meals as meal times, so he carried the wet grains, now fermented, to the sows. The following morning Lijah was first in the yard and saw the sows lying four in a row in the pen peacefully sleeping. Without a word to George Hedgecock, he nipped over the road and fetched Harry.

"Them sows a thine be as drunk as Lords."

"So bist thee," Harry said as he wiped his nose with his spotted handkerchief.

"Come and see then," Lijah laughed. "A fine stockman thee bist."

Both men prodded and slapped the fat sides of the sows but they slept on. "I'll tell the gaffer," said Harry. He met George Hedgecock coming through the dairy.

George laughed. "They'll be all right after dinner. Put some water in the trough and keep them off the beer today."

The sows, a bit wobbly, drank pure water after dinner and Lijah teased Harry. "Thee mind unt on thee work, no doubt you fancies another night alongside Esther."

At Croome Court Esther suckled Moses Steel and George,

Lady Coventry's son. Her little Lucy was now five years old, and David as a page boy at the great house was quite a young man at ten. He drove the little pony and cart to Worcester for the post, cleaned the boots and shoes and made himself generally useful about the house. Lord and Lady Coventry went to the Hunt Ball at Worcester and then by coach to London to meet the nobles and their ladies at dinner and at the theatre. They even met King George himself at a grand banquet and discussed farming and estate management with him.

That month before Christmas, Esther was well looked after, and the chaise fetched Harry and Tom over on Sundays when they could be spared from Sundial Farm.

Christmas came with flurries of snow and the poor of Ayshon shivered under thatch and stone tile, but Esther had her Moses and the remarks Lijah made to Harry brought a twinkle to his eye. As Lijah's rosy face shone on George Hedgecock's cider and his bristly chin dropped showing a gap where two teeth should have been, his waistcoat continually unbuttoned and his belly supported by his leather belt, he taunted Harry, winking an eye and saying, "It unt all on us a got thur missus a living at Croome Court."

On Christmas Day George Hedgecock and Mark were up early and did the feeding. Mark went around the stock on Bredon Hill and Harry rode George Hedgecock's hunter over to Lord Coventry's to spend the day with his wife. He took Tom on the tandem saddle.

Richard Surman and his mother entertained the poor of the parish to dinner, giving each one a shilling. They were regaled with roast goose, the men drank strong beer and the women shared some Madeira with Mrs Surman, who had boiled plum puddings and made apple pies served with cream. Surman and his mother did well by the poor that day, and next morning the

Archdeacon came to the curate's house to dole out the charity money. Jack Baker asked him for a new smock frock which, as sexton and clerk, he required. The year was almost through. A lot had happened in Ayshon and Beckford. Most important, Esther had given birth to another Moses and was rearing another Farmer George.

CHAPTER FOUR
The Comings and Goings of 1771

George Hedgecock's Horses and the Farrier

GEORGE HEDGECOCK was first and foremost a horseman, a horse breeder, and the farming side of him followed. Lijah, besides ploughing and sowing, bred foals from George Hedgecock's mares as he had done at Cosgrove in the Cotswolds. As Flower, Daisy and Dolly (George Hedgecock's mares) were stinted by the village stallion, the big black horse with white feathered fetlocks, they foaled usually in May or June. Now George Hedgecock was no horse coper, not the kind of man to take horses for sale. He worked them and tried them in all gears until they were four or five years old and then sold them to the merchant men of the Midlands. These men came yearly to Stow Fair, then walked long lines of haltered heavy horses, tied nose to tail, to the industrial towns where they pulled loads of coal and corn through cobbled streets. But if George saw a useful two-year-old in the market, or on a local farm, he would break it in and sell again at Stow.

In 1770 the village farrier at Ayshon was Henry Stokes. His main business was shoeing horses but he was often sent for by Squire, parson or labourer for drawing aching teeth. Harry, brother of Lord Waterford's bailiff, was equipped with crude pincers and fulfilled this extra office just as farriers in other villages did. A man who relieves pain is looked on as a benefactor just as much as the man who relieves poverty, but Henry Stokes relieved both. In the collection of Major P. I. C. Payne of Darlingscott, Warwickshire, there is a letter from a native of Ayshon imprisoned at Gloucester Castle in January 1770. His crime was probably no more than debt, but in the village farrier he had a friend indeed. He wrote as follows to Mr Henry Stokes of Ayshon, Blacksmith, "to be left at Mrs Sarah Bishop's, hat-maker in High Street, Tewkesbury, Gloucester—Mr Bishop, if you please to send this as usual you will oblige a friend to your brother".

Gloucester Castle, January 30th 1770

Gentlemen,

   I received your letter and thank you very kindly for the lining of it for there is hardly any thing more welcome now than clean stockings, clean straw, a clean shirt and a shilling. But I am afraid I shall not answer your expectations at this time for my spirits are sunk so low I fear I shall have great trouble to raise them high enough for poetry as I have nothing but water to drink.

> The Poets have in Ancient Times
> Said Water helped them in their Rhymes.
> Most certainly, it no[w] dos fail
> And is not half so good as Ale.
> For Water always makes the Fancy
> Too Dull to Write of Sall or Nancy.
> But if my Brain with Beer was fired,
> With writing I should ne'er be tired.
> But you must take it as it is
> And Pardon what you find Amiss.
> But lest that you should chance to think
> I want for nothing else but Drink,
> I think it very fit to tell ye
> I sometimes want to fill my belly.
> With Pudding, Bacon or with Beef
> Or Bread and Cheese would suit my teeth
> But as I often of this lack,

I then must eat a dish of Whack*
But if the Whack be wanting too,
I nothing have for teeth to do.
But say I'm Sick and Stomach nice
And away I go to kill my lice.
For though of all things else we're scanty
I do assure you, lice are plenty

*Whack is a Dish in great use here and is made with Water, Oatmeal, Salt and Treacle boiled and about as thick as pap.

The Hedgecock family thought well of Henry Stokes, the blacksmith at Land Close, and indeed all Ayshon admired the man.

At Stow Fair, George Hedgecock was known well for his honest dealing. He was breeding in Ayshon a most useful type of cart-horse for the clay lands. Lijah sat up in the stable with the brood mares as they foaled at Sundial Farm. Carrying his horn lantern he was quick into Hedgecock's loose box to tie the cord of the newborn foal as the mother licked away the mucus, head to tail.

George found Mark a chip of the old block — recognising a good animal and fast becoming a good judge of horseflesh. Tilda Hedgecock, with her sister Catherine, made a pretty picture as they rode sidesaddle on their hunters. When Harry Steel had trouble with straying stock, the girls were eager to help him drive them back to Sundial Farm. The Hedgecock twins hunted fast and fearless over Bredon Hill. Greg Trusswell became more and more a familiar visitor at the farm, courting Mathilda when he was on furlough. Lijah warned the girls and Greg about their hard riding on Bredon Hill. He spoke particularly to Tilda who rode a three-year-old mare.

"Once you a broke her wind, ur's finished and done for. You

have a good bred un under ya and without you a thinking I'm taking liberties, you'm no small weight for that mare to carry up Bredon Hill.''

"You're jealous of Greg, Lijah," Tilda giggled back at him, throwing her black hair across one shoulder.

"Certain," Lijah stammered back, feeling all the time he was speaking out of turn, "I thinks more of you two girls than all Master Hedgecock's horses. Greg ull have pleasanter nights along of you than I gets along of the father's mares. 'Tis none of my business, Miss Hedgecock, but I can't help noticing that Catherine ull be bespoke afore long.''

"Who by ?" Tilda liked teasing Lijah.

"Oh," said he, "the man as stands in St Andrew's pulpit most Sundays— the Rev. Richard Surman— B.A., unt he ?''

Tilda Hedgecock didn't keep Lijah guessing long, for at that very moment Richard Surman and Catherine came through the orchard hand in hand, then through the back door into the parlour for tea at Sundial Farm. Tilda giggled and Lijah raised his eyebrows. "Oi,"— and he got his pipe going with a twig of bramble still burning where he and Harry had lit a heap of hedge croppings that morning— "Miss Tilda to marry a soldier, Miss Catherine a parson. Master Hedgecock's daughters be worthy of good men. I wishes you bwoth the best. No man had a couple a finer daughters, to be sure.''

Births, Deaths and Marriages

When Lady Coventry's son, George, was weaned, Esther Steel returned from Croome Court to her wattle and daub cottage. Esther took this as a matter of course and was glad to be back on Harry's mattress, glad to see Anne Hedgecock busy in the dairy with her two daughters. Lijah and Jane welcomed home their neighbour with young Moses.

Lijah's rotund belly could no longer be contained in his waistcoat as he strutted around the rickyard with George Hedgecock, nosing into looseboxes, passing judgment on mares and foals. Lijah, breeder with Hedgecock of useful cart horses, gave more the impression of a stud groom working for a racehorse owner than that of a farmer's waggoner. Lijah, just a rosy-cheeked, broken-mouthed, wrinkled country chap, was a proud man, and had reason to be pleased with his success. The ashplant he walked with gained him some respect from the village lads who hung around his stables.

George Hedgecock was doing well at Sundial. His stock thrived, his men were loyal.

"How be the ship on the Common?" Lijah asked Harry one morning in the barn before Hedgecock came out with the orders for the day.

"They thrives on the limestone," Harry replied as he fed the milking cows another pitchforkful of hay. "Besides, you a got some useful horseflesh around the orchard. Dos't ever work any a them feathery legged horses a yourn?"

Lijah drank a mug of cider from the barrel and poured one for Harry (Hedgecock had given him this privilege). "Work um! they be allus at work at two year old. Thy bwoy Tom ull tell ya, we puts um in all gears. Then the cottage farmers borrows um to work their strips and a course at five year old Master Hedgecock sends the best warranted good workers in all gears to the city, coming back with his bag of sovereigns. Sometimes half a sovereign for me, but don't thee tell Jane; that's put by for a rainy day. How's Moses and Esther now they be back under thee own thatch?"

Harry gave a wry smile, smacked his lips over the last dregs in the cider mug, then almost in a whisper so that the Hedgecocks didn't hear he said, "As fat as butter. Esther's got lovely ways since her bin at Croome. I'll have to be careful or else there ull be two more christenings a coming off."

"Dall it, Harry, Moses a bin christened."

"Bist thee blind, Lijah? When you be tending to the mares and often in the dairy, can't you see that George Hedgecock's foot a slipped and Anne's in the family way?"

Lijah stood dumbfounded until he seemed to read of some invisible calendar that Anne was forty-three and the youngster would be what the gentry called 'an afterthought'. "What you might call a Cuckoo Lamb," he said. "A lamb born late, born when the cuckoo hoots from the topmost branch of the old oaks in Church Close in May."

At that moment Hedgecock walked into the barn.

"Sad news to tell you men. Archdeacon Trusswell's wife died yesterday. Died without issue at fifty-eight, same age as his Reverence."

"What does that myun, Gaffer? Without issue?" Lijah's face wrinkled still more with curiosity.

"Barren, you would call it," George Hedgecock said.

"Another job for Jack Baker the sexton. Still, it's all sand at Beckford churchyard, easy digging," Harry observed.

"Life is a continual coming and going," George Hedgecock went on with some feeling. "We are expecting an increase this year."

"Congratulations, Gaffer," Hedgecock's men said both together.

Three days later Emma Trusswell was buried in Beckford churchyard. For many years she had kept house for the Archdeacon and she had become his wife not so long before, a quiet wedding in Gloucester Cathedral performed by the Bishop himself. Ayshon was represented at her funeral by Lady Sarah, George Hedgecock and family, Stephen Bostock and Phil Besford. Richard Surman conducted the burial and the bearers were all Beckford men, men whose ancestors had tilled the soil for centuries.

The death of Mrs Trusswell postponed the marriage of Tilda Hedgecock and Gregory Trusswell. Hedgecock thought, as did the Archdeacon, that as a mark of respect the couple should wait another three months. These soon passed and in no time at all Mathilda went up St Andrew's aisle on her father's arm. Anne Hedgecock was, in Lijah's words, "looking close to profit". He could not take his mind off farm animals and farming ways even for this one day when the village orchestra played from the musicians' gallery as they had never played before. Tilda looked her loveliest in her wedding gown and Gregory was smart and upright in his uniform, with another young officer as best man. Lijah and Harry wiped tears from the corner of their eyes realising that Tilda would be joining her husband, perhaps in some distant land. They had seen her grow up from a baby.

After the ceremony, George Hedgecock entertained the gentry of Ayshon and some from Beckford in the large front drawing room at Sundial Farm—Lord Waterford, Lady Waterford, Lady Sarah Fitzwilliam and her beautiful twenty-one-year-old daughter, Dorothy, and Archdeacon Trusswell, a lone figure so recently bereaved. Hedgecock was already making a mark in Ayshon's village life. He not only farmed well, he bought and sold well, he lived well—"A man who never abuses himself," so Lijah described him.

From deep down in his pocket George drew out a sovereign for Proctor Perkins to entertain the cottage farmers, the squatters, the tradesmen, the labourers and the paupers that evening in the

Plough. Lijah's tongue, loosened by Perkins's best beer, entertained the company as he reminisced about his own wedding.
"Dalled if that wasn't a job, I couldn't wait for Jane to get her
stockings off, now thur's plenty a time for her to knit a pair.
Excuse me, Mam," he said to mug-washing Mrs Perkins behind
the bar, "we be just talking about nature." "So I gather," Mrs
Perkins replied, adding a few more mugs. "And you'll either
have to spend the night on the straw in Proctor's stable or some
of the stronger men will take you home to an angry Jane and
then you'll know who hasn't got their stockings off."

By now the Bakers and the rest of the village orchestra had
joined the company at the Plough, playing merry music to some
of the younger village folk who danced on the gravel under the
sign of The Plough. Lijah reclined in Proctor Perkins's inglenook, snoring away and dreaming of young Jane at Cosgrove
many moons ago. His rosy face now shone scarlet in the glow of
the fire, his unbuttoned waistcoat exposed a full and contented
belly, covered by his rough hair shirt.

"Let him bide," Bernard Baker said as he came in to lax his
thirst, "and I'll take him hwom. I can handle Jane, or perhaps
that's the wrong word for a man at my time a life — talk to her,
I myuns."

Next morning as Tom Steel drove the four-horse plough team
for Lijah in Staights Furlong, it was a gawmless looking ploughman he saw holding the plough tails. As they ate their bait under
the hedge, Lijah confessed that he had a "thick yud that morning
and don't seem to fancy the fittle in me frail. I wish that I could
follow the gaffer's pattern. George Hedgecock never abuses
himself like I did last night. Tom, did many of my secrets come
out at the Plough?"

"No, not as I heard, but Bernard Baker undressed you last
night and Jane was just in time when you throwed both of your

heavy boots on the kitchen fire afore you went to bed," said Tom.

"Ah, 'tis bad, Tom lad," Lijah spoke soft and low, " 'Tis bad when a man can't carry his liquor."

Then at nightfall, as Hedgecock's team were stabled, George, looking at Lijah, understood when he was told, "I be mortel sorry but we ain't ploughed an acre today."

"Never mind," said George Hedgecock, "there's another day tomorrow—and Mark, you are man enough to take another team and with Sam Parson's lad strike another bed on the ridge and furrow of Staights Furlong, Lijah will show you how."

Lijah straightened his back replying, "If we can't plough it between us, we'll make it nobody else can."

CHAPTER FIVE

Hawthorn-hedged Ayshon

Enclosure 1773

AFTER LOSING Emma, Archdeacon Trusswell turned more attention to the working of his glebe land and spent a lot of his time wining and dining with Lord Waterford at Beckford Hall. They discussed the wasteful way some of the farmland was being worked.

"Take Bernard Baker of Ayshon, for instance," Trusswell said to Waterford over a dinner of larded partridge. "Baker's got four strips of arable, each about one-third of an acre. One strip lies at the top of the Groaten, another halfway to Umberlands Lane, and then two together over the fence by Hedgecock's walnut tree. Mark my word, your Lordship," the Archdeacon went on, "enclosure must come as it has come already in some other parts of Britain."

The following Sunday the Archdeacon took the service at Ayshon Church. His eyes scanned the pews and aisles. There were Lady Sarah Fitzwilliam and Dorothy in their private pew— the manorial pew—accessible by its own private south door; the Rev. Phil Besford, Stephen Bostock, both sizeable farmers; George Hedgecock and family, of course; then the cottage farmers, Bakers, Bradfields, Allens, Parsons and so on. In the centre aisle sat the few tradesmen, masons, carpenters, wheelwrights, the publican, grooms, bailiffs and so on, then by the door the labourers in their smocks, the shepherds with their dogs. Trusswell thought how prudent it was for society still to have peasants who could be treated almost like the slaves who were being shipped from the African coast to the Indies to work in the plantations. His mind was bent on enclosure for two main reasons. Firstly, he resented the cottage farmers—the men who worked part time for his tenants or for Lord Waterford's, like Stephen Bostock.

"These men," he told his Lordship, "are idle some days during the week when they are supposed to be working their strips. They graze a cow on the common, a few geese, a sow and litter of pigs in Ayshon Wood. They become independent. Some," he said, "would put a half fat calf in the market then spend the money on drink." The second reason Trusswell had for enclosure was simply that the land could be worked more economically; that lots could be put together, the common fenced and grazed and divided among the people who had common rights.

Lord Waterford went part of the way with Trusswell's ideas but did spare a thought for the smallholders whose ancestors had had their strips, their grazing rights, since time immemorial. Lady Sarah Fitzwilliam too had doubts as to the prudency of enclosure, but she was in some small way committed by the engagement of her daughter Dorothy to the Hon. John Franklin, Lord Waterford's son and heir.

John Franklin, in his early twenties, had an eye to the future—to the future of the two villages, to the future of the land—without much thought for the small holder, whether he remained a little independent with his rights or became a common labourer at his master's beck and call, at the parson's beck and call, at the Squire's beck and call. Sir John was not ruled by sentiment; he thought of the land as so much grain, so much butter, so much beef and mutton. He agreed with his father about the points at issue. "For instance," he said, "how can land be worked crossways when the strips are only eleven yards wide? Then think of the waste on the headland, the damage by horses and oxen ploughing the strips and turning on the end of the one adjoining, trampling the land and crops."

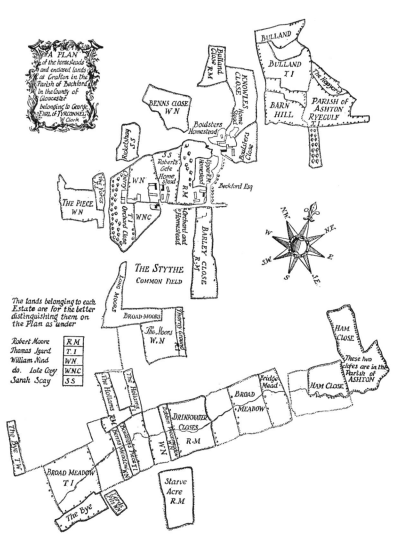

A PLAN of the homesteads and enclosed lands at Grafton in the Parish of Bechford in the County of Gloucester belonging to George EARL OF TYRCONNEL W Clark

BULLAND

BULLAND
T I

BARN HILL

The Hoppens

PARISH OF ASHTON RYEGULF
T.I

Bulland Close R.M

KNOWLES CLOSE

Home Stead

BENNS CLOSE W N

Boulsters Homestead

Boulsters Close

Ricketsbury S S

Cherry T I

The Floors

W N

Roberts Gate Home Stead S S

Upper R.M Homestead

Orchard Close T I

WNC

Orchard and Homestead

Beckford Esq

THE PIECE W N

BARLEY CLOSE R.M

THE STYTHE COMMON FIELD

Long Moors

BROAD-MOORS

The Moors W. N

Thorny Ground

HAM CLOSE

These two closes are in the Parish of ASHTON

HAM CLOSE

The lands belonging to each Estate are for the better distinguishing them on the Plan as under

Robert Moore	R.M
Thomas Izard	T.I
William Nind	W.N
do. Late Copy	W.N.C
Sarah Scay	S.S

The Hollams R.M

The Hollams T.I

Boulsters Mead T.I

Farms Meadow W.N

Robin Accreption

W.N

DRINKWATER CLOSES R.M

BROAD MEADOW

Fridge Mead

The Bye T.W

BROAD MEADOW T.I

Starve Acre R.M

The Bye

W
N.W
N.E
E
S.W
S.E
S

Grafton pattern, 1770

Harry Holmes, carter under Bailiff Stokes, and Tom Bosley, shepherd to Lord Waterford under Stokes, brought the news of the proposed enclosure to the Plough at Ayshon. They themselves had nothing to lose—no grazing rights, no strips—except that they did fire their bread ovens, when they had a little flour to bake bread, with faggots of gorse off Furze Hill, which would be cleared and enclosed if Enclosure was put into force.

Proctor Perkins talked with his customers in the Plough. He didn't favour enclosure; his regulars included quite a few independent smallholders who were a source of trade. Bernard Baker and Jim Bradfield declared that "Thur's no smoke without fire".

When Sir John Franklin married Dorothy Fitzwilliam, Lord Waterford retired with his wife to a large house in Beckford known as The Towers. Sir John and Lady Franklin then moved to the Hall. This move suited Archdeacon Trusswell; he could talk to young John Franklin as he could not talk to his father, and now Lord Waterford's son was Squire at Beckford while his mother-in-law was Squire at Ayshon.

Over a glass of port at the Red Lion at Beckford, a company of gentlemen met to carve up Beckford and Ayshon. Sir John Franklin, the chief landowner, in close consultation with the Archdeacon, had chosen as Commissioners Thomas Brown and Gilbert Jones, described as Gentlemen. They were appointed to divide the land. Jephcot, a professional gentleman from Northampton, was nominated as Clerk to the Commissioners.

The 22nd of June 1773 was the date decided upon to put the Act of Parliament into force and implement enclosure. This gave the folk of both villages a little time to stake their claim for land. The formal notice to this effect was nailed on St Andrew's Church door at Ayshon and St John's at Beckford. The notice read to the effect that the landowners would be entitled to the rights and privileges exercised and enjoyed by their ancestors and

also Royalties. It was intended to enclose all Common Fields and
Lot Grounds. Those people who held Common Rights and had
strips of arable would be allotted a distinct parcel of land if they
applied by a given date. Tithes to go to the Rev. Phil Besford and
Sir John Franklin. All old enclosures to be honoured and old
bargains at New England, between the parishes. Lady Sarah
Fitzwilliam to be allotted another one hundred acres adjoining
Sundial Farm, for George Hedgecock to farm as tenant.

Claims came in to the Commissioners from those cottage
farmers who understood the notice. As far as possible, strips of
arable were joined together into plots of no more than two acres
for the small farmers, but the snag was the fencing of the
Common. The small men who appealed for shares in Ayshon's
ground found themselves liable for a substantial amount of the
cost of fencing the Common, strip fields and meadow lands.
Rowdy meetings of the small cottage farmers at the Plough
proved useless.

The cottage farmers could see that it might be better to sell
out their rights to the landowners rather than pay fencing costs.
Jim Bradfield said, "I be gwain to claim my two acres"; Bernard
Baker said, "So be I, my Grandad worked my strips." "But you
won't have the same ground," Sam Parsons said. "They be
gwain to put the strips anant one another." Job Allen and Sam
Parsons never even staked their claim but, with the support of
their wives and families, spoke to Richard Surman about it.
Surman, that good man of Ayshon, approached the Archdeacon,
who declared that if Allen and Parsons refused to help to pay for
fencing, they could no longer be occupiers of land under the new
system. It was only to be expected that Sam Parsons riddled the
notice on St Andrew's church door with a shot from his blunder-
buss. Jack Baker, the parish clerk, knew who had done the
mischief but kept the news from Trusswell.

8

The meeting was held to divide the land. Bernard Baker and Jim Bradfield had two acres apiece next to each other in the Groaten; Archdeacon Trusswell had Little Hill; Phil Besford was allocated Furze Hill, giving Abel Smith the Methodist enough bush burning to last a life time; Sir John Franklin was to have the Wynch; and the Lower Groaten and Carrants Field went to the Archdeacon; Phil Besford had the Dewrest.

More men lost their rights at Ayshon than at Beckford. At Ayshon many more of the older men—older than Job Allen and Sam Parsons—lost their rights. They sold their cows and their geese and became labourers on and under the Hill. One man was happy—George Hedgecock, with his extra hundred acres to rent off Lady Sarah, became Ayshon's model farmer. Furthermore, his wife bore him another son the day after. "We'll call him Andrew," George said. "St Andrew's have treated us well with the enclosure."

After Job Allen and Sam Parsons and other cottage farmers had lost their land and spent the money they had received at the Plough, they became uneasy. Working every day for one man was not their mode of life, and work they would not until their little bit of savings were spent. As Francis Stokes supervised the fencing of John Franklin's estate, including Ayshon Wood where the timber came from, Allen and Parsons walked Bredon Hill at night, armed with axes, knocking down fences and breaking gates, but only on Franklin's land and Trusswell's land. "Besford and Hedgecock be good to the poor, we won't harm them," they said. The village constables were called out, but Allen and Parsons were too clever until one night Franklin's ricks were burnt down and Trusswell's barn burnt at the same time. It was the work of Sam Parsons alone, Job Allen being blind drunk in the Plough that night. Caught at last by the constables, Parsons first appeared at Beckford Court, where Archdeacon Trusswell, as Chief Magistrate, sent him to Gloucester Assize. Found guilty of firing ricks and a barn, endangering life, he was sentenced to be hanged at Gloucester Castle.

A gloom fell over Ayshon village the day Sam Parsons rode in the death cart to be hanged in Gloucester. The enclosure had claimed one man's life. Sam could not, nor would not, work for Squire or Parson. His great-grandfather had kept a cow on the common, a pig in the wood, grown barley on his strip.

The Archdeacon never preached in St Andrew's church again. The feeling against him ran high. Richard Surman told the congregation that times were changing and he would make it his business that the labourers were justly paid. Baker and Bradfield still had a measure of independence but could no longer keep a cow on the Common. The labourers themselves got so inflamed against Trusswell over the hanging of Sam Parsons that they too pulled down his fences until at last he had to get his men to dig ditches to mark his boundary, then plant hawthorn on the banks.

Nevertheless, enclosure at Ayshon and Beckford had gone off comparatively quietly. Neighbouring villages nearer Gloucester, where wages were low, protested and rioted, burning whole rickyards full of stacks. Seven shillings a week just didn't keep body and soul together, so poaching became rampant. Two brothers the other side of Bredon Hill were hanged at Gloucester for poaching, using arms against a keeper. One had a pregnant wife, an infant on her knee and another at the breast. "Better to hang than starve," labourers said as they drew their 2s 6d a week parish relief and poached nightly. The Plough at Ayshon became a source of poverty and the poor rate. As Job Allen said, "If I'm sober shall I be able to keep a cow or grow taters? No, bring me another pint." Families lived on bread and potatoes; the Game Laws caught up with some of the poachers— some were whipped, others sentenced to seven years' transportation to Australia.

Not all the villagers' lives were affected. Ayshon's carpenter and undertaker continued to work for 1s 6d a day. He wrote in a bold hand and made out his bills in a facetious manner:

Jan 9th 1799 — A coffin made for Sam Harris due to me from Ayshon Parish nine shillings

Apr 5th 1799 — Received of Mr Martin the contents of above nine shillings

John Bayzland — John a coffin I have made and the money I have received on 16th May — Mr Proctor did the money pay. John Bayzland did receive the same, and thought himself not much to blame.

Feb 28th 1780 — For a coffin for Thos Newman, this parish owes me tis thrice nine shillings, which is just my due.

The Parish Doctor received seventeen shillings, the payment to cover: Tincture 2s, Bolus 3s, Tincture 2s, Visits 5s, and the Church Warden carefully noted his expenses:

Visitation of Bishop		17/–	
Horse and Groom		1/–	
Dinner		3/9	
Bread, wine and washing linen 1782/83/84	£3	9	3
Barrel of lime for church		2/–	
Pews and doors, Tewkesbury		3/–	
6 nails of Irish cloth to repair surplice		?	
44 doz sparrows at 2d doz		7/4	

1782			
Shroud for Rich. Baker child		7/4	
Wm Baker ringing the bell and digging grave		2/6	
Mending the parish gun		4d	
Powder, shot, gates, stiles, mounding	£3	11	10

1784

Expenses with the bells at Tewkesbury, taking and fetching	16/6
Going to Gloucester to argue with Mr Rushall	9/–

The Church, under Richard Surman at St Andrew's, survived enclosure. The Methodists still met in a part of Ayshon Wood around the house which Jonah Stubbs was allocated in 'The Award'. Ayshon folk, that is to say, the ordinary villagers, continued to feel very sore about the hanging of Sam Parsons for his confessed fire raising. Surman helped Sam's widow and George Hedgecock employed his thirteen-year-old son. Sam was only one example of the people of 1773. He had held grazing rights on the Common as his ancestors had done from time immemorial. He always cultivated his strips and, being an uneducated man, he deemed it robbery to deprive him of part of his livelihood. In fact it was robbery, but legal robbery. He had not the know-how or the spirit to stake his claim, and had stubbornly refused to pay for fencing the Common for others' benefit apart from his own. Sam had no great ambition; he just wanted to live his life as he had always done. If Sam's life and work were not producing the maximum from Ayshon's soil, what of it, he thought. Six days ruled by the Squire and one day by Archdeacon Trusswell would leave him no time, no right to cultivate his strip, to keep his pig. Enclosure would no doubt produce more food from Britain's acres, but what of the labouring classes who not only stood to lose their independence and some of their income, but were being put at the complete mercy of the ruling classes? To have no share at all in the improved farming of the land; to stand outside their cottages, little better than pig styes, living on bread and green stuff—meat being a luxury, to see their children go hungry, no more to roam the woods for firewood or gather gorse

from Furze Hill. . . . As the Ayshon men worked in wind, sun
and rain, as the eight threshing floors in the tall timbered barns
resounded from harvest until May with the crack of the flail on
the threshing floors as sixteen men beat out with their double
sticks the corn from the ear, as other men winnowed with the
wooden shovels in draughty doorways, Ayshon was no longer a
part of Merrie England. George the Third's administration had
made for a more efficient agriculture but not a happier one. It
had now become difficult, well nigh impossible, for a farm
labourer to climb higher up the farming ladder.

The Plight of the Labourers

Bernard Baker and Jim Bradfield paid the fencing charges after
enclosure and maintained their independence. As for the rest of
the Ayshon cottage farmers—Job Allen and his neighbours—
they eventually had no option but to work full time for the
Squire, the parson and the Hedgecocks. Job Allen, time and time
again, regretted his decision to give up his arable strip and sell
out, but he agreed that there was no future in it if he couldn't
graze a cow on the Common and cut turf and gorse on Furze Hill
for firing. Ayshon became a cold place for the labourers of the
fields in Winter. Richard Surman was angry when he heard a
Member of Parliament suggest that the labourers and their
families should quit their hovel-like cottages in Winter and sleep
in byres with the cattle in order that the heat generated by the
beasts would give them warmth.

George Hedgecock alone in Ayshon considered the plight of his
seven shillings a week men. He even went to the trouble of working out a budget of how the money *could* maintain a family. Anne
Hedgecock saw that none of the families on her husband's farm

went short of milk. Job Allen and his friends poached Bredon
Hill regularly, taking note when the gamekeepers and constables
were at the Plough. The Bradfields and Bakers were not allowed
to trap game on their two acre strips, so apart from their wheat
and barley, they were only a little better off than the labourers.

Since Phil Besford had enclosed Furze Hill and cleared the
gorse to graze his cattle, the only people who had legal rights
for firing wood were the hedge-cutters in Winter. They were
allowed to take home a faggot or kid of hedge trimmings each
night, bound with a withy twig, but it was insufficient for firing
the bread ovens even if the labourers had bread to bake. Corn
prices soared, wheat in particular. The squire and his tenants
forbade the labourers' wives and children to glean after harvest.

Job Allen, who had spent his bit of compensation money
when he gave up his arable strip, remarked at the Plough to
Harry, Lijah and the rest: "We beunt allowed to get firing out
of Ayshon Wood, nor faggots of gorse off Furze Hill — that's
warmth we be without. Now they a stopped the missus and kids a
gleaning. What be us to live for? Slaving our guts out for seven
shillings a week. Best nail up the privvy door, if we can't yut,
we shan't want the privvy."

Richard Surman made one of his infrequent visits to the Plough
that evening and quoting from Leviticus 19, verse 9, said that he
read there: "And when ye reap the corners of thy field, neither
shalt thou gather the gleaning of the harvest."

"Thur ya be, the curate knows the Old Testament, we be
gwain against the Almighty." Job's beery breath came right
against the curate's face as he added, "Didn't Ruth glean along
uv her mother in law? — leaze we calls it in Gloucestershire, but
it's the same thing."

"Now Job, Lijah and Harry, how much corn did your family
reckon to gather gleaning in the past?" Surman asked.

"Oi, enough to kip us in bread best part of the year," Job replied. "I minds the time when the church bell was passed when the women started in the morning."

"Yes," Harry said, "it yunt long ago since they leazed enough byuns to fatten a pig for ourselves."

"Thy mind's allus on bacon, lard and chitterlings," said Lijah putting his thumbs in the armholes of his waistcoat. Puffing at his clay pipe he finished the conversation with, "It's the wheat we wants to feed the missus and kids." Mr Surman looked thoughtfully into Perkins's fire. He thought of the thousands of bushels of wheat being grown in Gloucestershire and Worcestershire; how this wheat at high prices was feeding the people of the Black Country, much of it going on the waterways north for the iron masters, their men, the mechanics and miners. He thought of his flock at Ayshon going hungry and how willing the womenfolk would be to glean every ear of wheat, how the children would collect the wood if they were allowed. He looked at Job and knew that, although Bredon Hill rabbits were one of the street cries of London, Job didn't have many meatless days. He knew, though, that Job couldn't afford butchers' meat and he now had no pig.

Lijah tipped his mug of beer and called for another and one for the curate. Richard Surman accepted but insisted on paying for all present; then he told them what had crossed his mind. "I'll preach about gleaning on Sunday. It may do good, it may touch their stony hearts," and with this he left the company at the Plough, admiring their spirit but doubtful about their lot improving.

The following Sunday, Surman's text was concerning Boaz and Ruth. The orders of Boaz to his men were: "And let fall some of the handfuls of purpose for her and leave (them) and rebuke her not."

George Hedgecock's heart was touched; he thought of the grinding poverty at Ayshon and turning to Anne after service declared: "Ayshon folk shall glean my cornfields. My labourers' wives shall have preference to the other villagers." Surman was pleased with George Hedgecock's thought for the poor but the Squire and his tenants left Ayshon church unmoved, sticking rigidly to the Enclosure Award of 22nd June 1773.

That harvest on George Hedgecock's farm, as soon as the sheaves were carried, the women and children flocked to the corn stubble, gathering up every ear of wheat in their hurden aprons, then home at nightfall as the sun settled behind the acorn-covered oaks where Elmley Castle abutted Ayshon on Bredon Hill.

Job Allen chuckled as the women and children came home with the scroggins as he called the gleaned corn. " 'Tis like gold," he told them as the Allens' share lay on the floor of his back kitchen. Then Job and his neighbours swung their flails on the stone flagged back yard in the moonlight deep into the night. The grain and chaff was sieved through rough withy riddles before the winnowing.

"Pity we don't live at A'sum," Job told his wife.

"Whatever for? Thur's nothing wrong with Ayshon when the youngsters don't have to go hungry."

"Just thinking of the winnowing, that was all," Job said. "It's uzzeyer at A'sum, they winnows the corn under the Bell Tower by the river. You see, thur's allus a draught through thur under the belfrey. All the men have to do is to turn the wheat and chaff together with wooden shovels and the wind blows all the chaff away leaving the wheat clean and ready for milling."

Job's wife pondered. She was tired, walking acres of Hedgecock's land for each bushel gathered. " 'Tis like the day of judgment the curate speaks of when the wheat shall be separated from the chaff. Still, let's get off to bed and lie for a few hours on the old chaff mattress that have eased our backs for many harvests. Morning ull come all too soon; you'll be pitching and loading sheaves, I'll be leazing the fallen ears.''

Archdeacon Trusswell who, with John Franklin, was architect of enclosure at Ayshon and Beckford, thought George Hedgecock was toadying to the labourers, their wives and families by allowing them the right to glean corn and thought Anne Hedgecock was being soft in allowing milk for the children on Sundial Farm.

One family who suffered from the new system of farming were the Pickfords. True, Fred Pickford never had an arable strip or grazing rights, but his family gleaned and got their firing for the bread oven off Furze Hill. After enclosure, Fred Pickford found Steve Bostock, his employer, as hard as nails. Wheat prices were high, every inch of available land was planted with corn. Bostock refused to sell any milk to Ayshon folk; he found that there was a ready market in the towns for veal, so his cows suckled their calves for about three months, then, sleek and fat, they were slaughtered to satisfy the taste of the city merchant and the wealthy gentry. Running the same risk as Job Allen, Fred poached on Bredon Hill and secretly took milk home to his hungry children.

The plight of the poor in Ayshon became the subject of the next Vestry Meeting. Beckford and Ayshon held a joint Vestry Meeting. The Archdeacon in his report told the people present how it had come to his notice that the labourers were objecting to bread made from barley and bean flour. "I have eaten this bread," he said. "They are taking more to tea drinking, apeing the gentry." Steve Bostock agreed, stating that Fred Pickford more than any insisted on bread made from wheaten flour and that he drank tea.

Richard Surman understood clearly that the landowners and tenant farmers were standing up for their rights but he was also aware of the labourers' plight. He told the meeting that George Hedgecock had set a good example in allowing the labourers to glean his stubble and collect a little fallen wood from the hedgerow trees. "We all know," the curate continued, "that this practice, if it spread to some of the farms, could lead to prosecution, public whipping and possibly public hanging. We don't want this to happen to the people of Ayshon."

"Give them an inch and they will take a yard," was Bostock's reply. "Besides, if the labourers leaze baskets of wheat the village baker will lose some of his customers."

Richard Surman had heard before the arguments about the barley bread. "I happen to know," he said, turning to the Archdeacon and John Franklin "that the people in the North of England eat the barley bread without complaint. The Scots live to a large extent on oatmeal, but there is a difference in Gloucestershire — a big difference. Bread in our part of the country is the mainstay of the labourer's diet, so he needs the best bread made from wheaten flour. What else does he get apart from turnips, potatoes, greens, meat — if he poaches? No milk. Milk cannot be bought in Ayshon even if the farm men had money to buy it. It's Master Bostock's affair if his milk feeds veal calves, but George Hedgecock provides milk for his men."

The Archdeacon looked at his curate in a way that Richard understood as well as if his thoughts had been expressed in words; thoughts that the man who worked under him as curate of St Andrew's was a radical. Trusswell snapped out: "Why do the landworkers in the North work contentedly on barley bread?" "Yes," Bostock butted in, "and drink tea kettle broth."

The two reverend gentlemen were puzzled by that remark and

Steve Bostock had to explain that it was a name sometimes given to burnt toast put into a basin with scalding water poured over it and a pinch of salt and pepper to taste. But Surman had good evidence to prove that the labourers on the land in the North spent money on milk, cheese and a little meat; that was why they were satisfied with their barley bread.

John Franklin thumped the oak vestry table exclaiming, "This is getting us nowhere, this tittle-tattle about whether the bread is made out of barley, wheat or sawdust. With wars and shortages, every acre must provide grain for our troops, our cities and so forth. I want to know why the Poor Rate has risen so much of late. It's three times as high as a few years ago."

The overseers, the clerk, the waywardens all had their say but it was Surman again who provided the answer. "First of all," he said, "you are keeping wages so low that large families have to depend on Poor Relief. Secondly, I hate to say this, some farmers are drawing labour from the Union and paying little for it. These men have to live on the Poor Rate. Then the roundman system has increased, especially in Winter. It means that men in this parish — six to my knowledge — go round from farm to farm doing a day's work, then on again. These men are not paid as much as the regular labourers so the difference is made up out of the Poor Rate. If only the farmers and landlords would realise that by paying their men a little extra the Poor Rate would drop."

John Franklin gave a deep sigh, rattling the golden coins in his breeches pocket. The Archdeacon said sulkily, "My curate has the answer for everything."

"But, sir," Richard replied, "the gentlemen of the Vestry Meeting are the ratepayers and employers. Surely our labourers would rather have wages than relief?" With this the meeting closed, but one thing was plain: that Ayshon would be a poorer place without Richard Surman and George Hedgecock.

Next day, although he was definite about keeping the gleaners off his stubble and forbidding the gathering of wood from his fields, Steve Bostock put a notice on his church door saying that he would give a reward to "labourers who shall bring up, or already have brought up, the biggest family of legitimate children without parish relief".

In the Plough that night there was a lot of leg-pulling towards closing time as Proctor Perkins's brew loosened the tongues and reddened the faces.

"What about thee, Lijah?" Harry said to his workmate.

"Well, I suppose as them as has the pleasure a getting youngsters should have the pleasure a keeping um." Lijah was quick with his answer, as quick as he was at doing up the two top buttons of his breeches to hold in that big belly of his. "Ever since Harry carried that titled 'ooman down Bredon Hill he a never bin the same. I udn't trust him no farther than I could spit. Now's your chance, Harry—they got to be 'gitimate, mind— none a this carrying on with George Hedgecock's servant girls in the cellar."

Harry straightened himself saying, "To yur thee talk anybody ud think that I was as bad as George Hedgecock's bull. It takes two to make a bargain. I've had my share but 'tis a challenge to the young couples. Bostock and his missus ain't made much of a show."

"Oh, but they beunt labourers." Fred Pickford, Bostock's ploughman, wasn't making any excuse for his employer—"just keeping the book straight," he said. "The gentry be like cock pheasants," Tom Bosley remarked, poking the fire with his shepherd's crook. "They don't stick to one henbird, they has several and when they travels a distance, say to London or Norwich or Bristol, and gets a girl in the family way, thur's no checking on um like say if I colted one at Beckford."

"I reckon it's a damned insult to human nature," was Harold Holmes's opinion. "Be we considered like Franklin's tups on Bredon Hill? Next thing Bostock ull want ull be to raddle our westcoats like they paints a ram's breast red."

Young Norman Bosley laughed as he said, "Thur ull be some big bellies up and down Ayshon village, I'll warrant. What's the prize?—not a lot if I knows Steve Bostock."

The customers stood awhile outside the Plough praising the curate for the stand he had taken at "the Vestry" and George Hedgecock for the kindness he showed his workers' families. What the labourers' wives said when their husbands told them of Bostock's offer was never known, but it would take more than a prize to bring children into a village that was poor and often hungry.

Richard Surman Ties a Knot

As the 1770s drew to a close and Enclosure ceased to be the chief talking point at the Plough, the Rev. Richard Surman and Catherine Hedgecock arranged their wedding at St Andrew's at Ayshon. Richard Surman's mother had become a little frail and there was ample room at the vicarage for the curate and his bride without interfering in any way with her comfort.

" 'Tis only right," Lijah Hicks said to Jim Bradfield as they both leaned against Proctor Perkins's five-barred gate outside the Plough yard.

"What bist a talking about?" Jim asked as puffs of blue smoke rose in little rings from their clay pipes in the still evening air.

" 'Tis only right for Master Richard to have a wife, and who better than Catherine? Her ull be as good as meat and drink to him. You be listening, Jim, to what I be saying? Bachelors when they becomes older develops peculiar habits and I have heard it said among the gentry that to remain chaste for too long causes the gout. Mind, my opinion is that it's just an excuse to have a randy with a London butterfly. Now our curate yunt like that, but that collar as he wears bachuds don't make his nature any different to ourn. In fact, 'tis more difficult for a parson to keep to the straight and narra. Without they farms, does a bit of work with their hands, hunts and shoots, they gets tempted.''

"What the nation bist on about?" Jim retorted with a well aimed spit across the yard.

Lijah was at no loss for words although Jim was not over-anxious to hear them. He went on: ''I bin talking to Abel Smith, the Methody. Abel says as how parsons be a sort of target for adventurous spinsters. They gives any young curate covetous looks from thur pews. They invites um to arternoon tay, encour-ages um with thur frilly and flouncy gowns on the sofa. They be supposed to restrain themselves like the Doctor does when he examines thur parts but 'tis a hazurd.''

"When Dick Surman's married, he ull have plenty to attend to at home with Catherine.'' Jim Bradfield thought of Richard Surman and Catherine Hedgecock, but most of all Lijah Hicks. His thoughts became words as he told Lijah quite plain how lucky it was for Ayshon village girls that Lijah had Jane at home; farm work—hard manual work—would not be enough to quench the fire in him.

The couple parted that night after a few mugs of Perkins's cider, meeting at St Andrew's the following Sunday morning to hear the Rev. Richard Surman, bachelor of this parish, and Catherine Hedgecock, spinster of this parish, asked in church, the banns being published for the first time.

As Lijah Hicks took a five-year-old gelding to Stow Fair, Prince out of Dolly, a brood mare, he pondered on Stanway Hill. The white webbing halter on Prince's head, new from the saddler, would be sold with the gelding. Henry Stokes had shoed the young gelding all round, blacking the top of the hooves with that mixture applied by the round brush used by the men of the farrier's trade. George Hedgecock passed Lijah on the Cosgrove Road they both knew so well. He was riding his heavy hunter to arrive at Stow Fair before Lijah and Prince. As Lijah viewed A'sum Vale from a Cotswold stone wall he thought of the wedding. "Sometimes," he thought, "we threshes a rick of corn to pay the rent money, sometimes we sells two or three young horses, you, Prince my beauty, be gwain to pay for Catherine's wedding."

Lijah was loth to part with his five-year-olds. "You see, they had just got handy." This was different. He whispered to Prince as they journeyed to the Fair on the Wolds: "Prince, you be to pay for a princess to marry our curate." No other words could describe Lijah's feelings for Catherine. Abel Smith had described her as like Caesar's wife, above suspicion. The horse was sold and George Hedgecock brought Lijah back with him on the tandem saddle. Archdeacon Trusswell, who had vowed never to come to Ayshon church again, arranged for Phil Besford to marry Richard and Catherine.

The wedding was celebrated in exactly the same way as Tilda's. The gentry refreshed themselves at Sundial Farm, the labourers and tradesmen at the Plough. But this time Jane Hicks kept a watchful eye on Lijah, getting him home "a little peart" but not drunk.

"He a tied a knot with his tongue he can't undo with his teeth," Lijah said to his wife as she helped him off with his boots. "I don't deny I be envious of such a fine piece," he said as he climbed the wooden stairs. "Thur's summat about George Hedgecock's daughters."

The Red Lion, Beckford, where a company of gentlemen met to carve up Beckford and Ayshon.

The Regulator at a spanking pace on the flat.

CHAPTER SIX

The End of a Century

The Follies 1797

ESIDES HIS improvements in the gardens and grounds of Croome Court—the building of little temples and bridges vying with the Follies which were the pride of Worcestershire—Lord Coventry's late father built a sham castle on Defford Common. This castle, constructed in 1750 in the pinky brown stone of the Malverns, stood at the very end of a mile-long avenue of trees, planted with such precision that they could only be described as two lines of soldiers of green-leaved elm, standing to attention to be reviewed by King George III himself. It seemed that not a leaf was out of place, not a branch marred the splendour of the parallel lines.

From the window of one of Croome Court's great drawing rooms, Lord Coventry would watch the varying moods of the sun playing tricks with the pink stone of the palace—as palace it was from a mile away, though close to just a trim improver of the flat Avon Valley landscape. Now old Lord Coventry's bones lay alongside his wife's in the family vault at Croome Court; the elms had grown but they still marked a green grass ride from the Court to Defford Castle. Harry Steel admired it greatly when he had visited Esther during her stay at the great house.

" 'Tis like fairyland," he told Master Hedgecock, "when you ride that straight mile cantering over springy turf. The Folly becomes more grand with the sun shining only on the tower, the trees shading horse and rider all the way."

The eighteenth century was drawing to a close. George III had been many years on the throne; his farming schemes, aided by the best brains in England, had produced good harvests but not always good prices. The labourers' lot was so bound up with the price of bread, the price of wheat. Their wages remained stable apart from a few pence.

Lijah Hicks talked of Follies to Abel Smith, still as an old man meeting with the Methodists in the wood. Lijah was growing old too but still ploughing and sowing. "Follies," said Abel, "be mentioned in the Word. Job 4.18 says: 'Behold he put no trust in his servants and his angels he charged with folly.' You see," said Abel, "the fool and his money be soon parted."

In the Plough the Bradfields and the Allens grew old, they talked of Harry Miles's death, the loss the curate had when old Mrs Surman died. One Spring evening Bernard Baker came into the Plough kitchen on two sticks, crippled with rheumatics, bent with age, weathered by ninety odd Summers and his blood thinned by the same number of sharp Winters.

"We be gwain to have a Folly on Bredon Hill," he announced to the company. "Not as it'll make any odds to me 'cause I shall be gone afore they have finished building him."

"Whose idea is it?" Fred Pickford asked.

"Mr Franklin's, of course; 'tis his land," gasped out Bernard leaning against a chair holding his mug of cider as he stood supported by one of his sticks, the other hooked over the chair back. "I shall never climb Bredon Hill again, but Harry Steel still keeps some sheep on the enclosure anant the Bambury Stones. Hedgecock rents that field off Lady Sarah; Mr John being her son-in-law is more or less landlord to Hedgecock now."

"Stonemason be already at work," Harry Steel confirmed as he and his tired sheep dog entered Perkins's house. Then he told how he had talked to Francis Stokes, Franklin's bailiff. "A scholar is Francis; he reads and writes and studies history. These Follies be all the fashion nowaday. The gentry builds 'em like their ancestors built the churches when they got money to spare, like the Cotswold sheep farmers built the wool churches out of their wool money."

Harry had his midday bait with the Masons in the shelter of the quarry. Then soon their chipping and hammering began once more as stones took shape, dressed in blocks in various sizes; dressed by the chisel but, with skill, no chisel marks could be seen. During the afternoon, Harry again walked round his flock wondering how many more times he would see the setting sun over the Malvern range, purple in the distance. "Never mind," he thought, "my bwoy Tom's a growing man. He can reap and tie and use a scythe. He will help me to trim the soiled wool of the hindquarters of the ewes with the belting shears. He will help me to shear. Ah, Tom's a bwoy to be proud on, Tom ull take over Hedgecock's sheep."

As he walked crook in hand, dog at heel, towards the Folly builders, he noticed a ewe's long fleece had been caught up in a blackberry bush. The bramble encircled its neck like a rope; how many times had Harry seen this? How many ewes had he turned over as they lay cast on their backs unable to regain their feet? "It's just another predicament they gets into before shearing time," he thought as he cut the briar with the shears he carried in a sheath on his belt. Two lambs stood bleating helplessly by and on her release the ewe ran off with her young leaving wisps of wool clinging to the briar.

As Harry neared the Folly, he saw the dressed stone mortared into place; a square tower made of Bredon Hill stone. The masons remarked on the view from the hill, Harry confided to them what Stokes, the bailiff, had told him: that the hill was 960 feet above sea level and the tower was to be forty feet high, that makes a thousand, don't it?"

"Ah, that's right. Forty feet we have orders to build it, battlemented with a flat roof. The stone steps inside through the doorway will wind their way atop," said the masons.

"That forty feet won't make much difference regarding the

view," Harry observed, "but it's to be a summer house for the
Lord of the Manor and his friends to have picnics here. 'Tis a
fine structure, different to some of the wattle and daub at
Ayshon," he continued. "It's a funny thing with the gentry, they
landscapes their gardens, they builds these Follies just to be
pleasing to the eye, but if the winter's gale blows the thatch off
the labourers' houses, that can wait— wait a devil of a long time.
I be lucky with Hedgecocks, they be good to the likes a me, but
Master, or should I say Mr John Franklin, don't care a cuss as
long as the work's done. Hovels some of his houses be, only fit
for pigs. Our womenfolk and the little uns at home suffers in
Winter. Still," Harry concluded, pulling his shepherd's smock
around his bent back, "one law for the rich and one for the
poor."

The Folly was completed sooner than had been expected; in
fact, it was old Bernard Baker himself who brought the news to
the Plough, though he was unable to climb Bredon Hill to see the
tower. No one was very interested. "The likes a we," Jim
Bradfield commented, "won't be invited up on top yet awhile.
No doubt Lord Coventry will be over with her Ladyship and son
George."

"Folly— a good name for it," was Fred Pickford's opinion.
"Buildings be meant to live in, worship in, or keep the corn in
and the cattle, ship and 'osses."

Bredon Hill Folly was John and Dorothy Franklin's pride and
joy. It was squat compared with Defford Castle, but its elevated
position gave it a commanding view over Avon Vale, over to the
Malverns, the Black Mountains, the Clee Hill and the Sugar
Loaf on a clear day. As Lord and Lady Coventry and George
hunted their packs of hounds they saw the work of the masons,
and Lady Coventry rather envied Dorothy Franklin.

That evening at dinner, she made it quite plain to her husband that she would like a Folly. As his Lordship tossed and turned on his bed, his mind wandered over his great estate. It stretched as far as the Cotswolds and beyond the Cotswold Edge, above Broddy (Broadway) village, towards where the sun rose, east of Croome. The address given by the vicar on the previous Sunday concerned Joseph— "And they said to one another, Behold this dreamer cometh" (Genesis 37, 16).

"The dreamer," Lord Coventry pondered.

> "We are such stuff
> As dreams are made on, and our little life
> Is rounded with a sleep. . . ."

The world, he thought, is shaped anew by dreams when dreamers can make their dreams come true. Some have dreamt of marble halls, some of terraced gardens, of lakes and bridges— and all at once Lord Coventry knew what dream of his, if it materialised, would give most pleasure to his wife: a battlemented tower, hexagonal in shape. Then he thought again— why not three towers like this, in the Gothic style? His dreams were taking shape as he decided on one hexagonal tower garnished with three circular towers.

There was hardly a limit to what Lady Coventry's husband would do to please her, and she was delighted by this idea for a Folly. After she had ordered fires to be lit on Broddy Hill so that she could see which site was best, the spot was chosen. In 1797, George's twentieth year as heir of Croome, the plans took shape. How often in centuries past men had dreamed of sculptured clustering pillars and lofty dim aisles before the builders had so much as hewn a stone or carved a piece of wood. These ancestors of Lord Coventry had no plans to work from but they constructed exactly what they wanted by marks in a lime pit. The masons at Broddy secured and buttressed their tower on the lofty windswept skyline hard by the London Road where men had hung from the gibbet, where highwaymen stopped the London to Worcester coach as it blunderbussed its way over the Cotswolds. First they made living quarters for the caretaker on the ground floor and first storey; these were built with chimneys and stairs. Then the tower went up apace—up into the clear Cotswold air, higher than anything for miles around, the fertile Vale of Evesham at its feet and a panoramic view of a dozen counties from its tower. Ayshon men saw it rise stone by stone; on clear days they could see the masons working. Richard Surman talked of greater temples, those not made with hands. He was a humble man, the curate, and like the Hedgecocks he delighted in the simple life. The hunt, the ball, the theatre were not for him; he chose instead to share the afflictions of the Ayshon labourers. As Broddy Tower was finished and the villagers spoke in whispers to him of the waste of money, Richard Surman said he was afraid it was still the Church's attitude to believe in 'The rich man in his castle, the poor man at the gate, He made them high and lowly and ordered their estate'.

"We shan't see this tower from Ayshon, mind tha," said Job Allen. "From the village it ull be hid by the knolp, by the parish quarry and the beech trees and the Great Hill Barn. Ecklington on the Avon will have the best view, but the part of the hill near the Bambury Stones can be seen from some parts of Beckford. Mr John ull see it from Beckford Hall."

Some days after, as Hedgecock's ewes and lambs grazed the Bambury Stone enclosure, the lambs gambolling over the limestone outcrop which some folk said was like an elephant, but never having seen an elephant, Harry said, "I won't say yes or no so I shan't be right or wrong." He took some time off his shepherding. He watched the masons, some at the quarry, some at the tower, until Mark Hedgecock, now a strong young man taking his father's place, climbed Bredon Hill and found Harry in the parish quarry.

"How are the lambs this morning, Harry? Is there enough grass for the ewes now or shall I send Tom Hicks up with another load of turnips?"

"Oh, we be all right for keep now—plenty of short sweet spring grass. The ewes be in fine fettle," Harry answered, looking sheepishly at Mark, knowing full well that Mark was not at all pleased to find him with the masons in the quarry instead of with his sheep. But Mark and Harry understood each other. Mark valued Harry's experience and he had no cause to find fault with the way he did his shepherding.

"Come on, Harry," said Mark. "Let's have a quiet walk around the flock. Tie the dog up to that hawthorn, then we can watch them graze."

So around the boundaries they took the usual stroll to see that every fence was in order, every gate fastened.

"These fences," Harry told Mark, "do charm my eyes, although they be getting dim. 'Tis here you see many young fledglings start to fly. Many's the time I have picked up a swift on a Spring day such as this, when he was lying helpless on the ground, his wings outstretched and his short legs unable to get him flying again. I've placed them on your fences, then away up into the heavens they go. Safe from the stoat, the weasel, the hovering hawk and buzzard."

" 'Tis nice to hear you talk so, Harry," Mark said tapping his stick against a bridle gate, tapping his stick and thinking deeply of how Harry considered all living things—how the woodbine blows, how the red streaks in it show against the grey sky, how it twines its stems around a young ash. The lambs still gambolled around the Bambury Stones; they seemed almost to be running organised races, as if they heard the word 'go' and off they

went to try their speed. The green turf gave off flurries of limestone dust as they bounded along. Then up the slope they went,
resting, indifferent to their bleating mothers, on some thyme
covered hillock. A leaf blown in the wind or a lark rising from
the ground set them off again along the age-worn tracks, scattering the flowering gorse as they ran back to their mothers for
milk. As the lambs, now so strong, suckled, bunting their heads
against the udder and pushing the ewes sideways in their tracks,
as the startled thrush shook a white shower of blossom from the
hawthorn bush and timid rabbits left their formes in the tufted
grass, Mark left Harry on the hill. A passing shower washed out
the footmarks where reynard had made his nightly round.

The masons' work went on apace. A few days after Bernard
Baker had lifted his eyes and seen the finished Broddy Tower, he
went to join his brother Charles, the late clerk, in temples not
made with hands.

So, with three years to go to complete the eighteenth century,
the prospect again changed on the age-old, tree-covered Broddy
Hill. As Jack Baker said when his old Uncle Bernard was buried
near St Andrew's tower at Ayshon, "It yunt quite as big a folly as
the t'other two—the bottom storeys do house a family."

The Thresher

As the eighteenth century drew to its inevitable close, it seemed
like Autumn, late Autumn, coming to Ayshon, as if the first cider
apples fell into the nettled turf and the velts were replacing the
swallows—but had not other centuries come and gone and
wouldn't there be more? Harvest follows seedtime as sure as
night follows day. But life's pattern in Ayshon had changed since
enclosure and not only because of it but despite it. Shepherd boys

no longer watched their sheep, whittling away the time with the old tunes. Sheep had become a saleable product; lambs grew fat on Bredon Hill turnips. Farmers like Hedgecock were quick to realise that wheat was the thing to grow in the vale fields; Britain being at war, then an uneasy peace, was hungry for grain. Old pastures were ploughed on Sundial Farm; land that had perhaps never before felt the lift of the ploughshare, the cut of the coulter. Lijah Hicks, a ploughman used to the awkward field, the sideland field, turned in the buttercup, the thyme, the clover, all the herbage, with his long wooden plough and four horses. George Hedgecock himself ploughed the stubbles with another team for barley the following Spring. Tom Steel ploughed some of the light hill grounds with the cunning of his Cotswold upbringing.

"Next Winter," Lijah told Proctor Perkins's customers one night in early Spring, "the two sticks ull be swinging ding dong in almost every barn in Ayshon a-thrashing Hedgecock's wheat." Lijah said this knowing full well that he would be swinging the flail following the harvest.

"That ull get rid of some of that belly a yours, Lijah," Proctor Perkins laughed as he wiped a pewter tankard.

Lijah was right in his prediction — it was a bumper harvest, well gathered and ricked and thatched. The first wet day, flails were brought down from off their dusty pegs in the chaff house by the stable. The joint where the short swingel stick fastened to the longer hand stick was of eel skin. Mark had been setting night lines, baited with worms from the steaming muck heaps of Sundial Farm, to catch the elusive eel. With age-old dexterity, Lijah, with waxed end thread, made the hinges for the two sticks or flails. George Hedgecock had two thrashers working with their flails in most of his barns, but at the Long Home Barn at Sundial Lijah worked alone. On Winter mornings before the cocks had crowed, a sign for some to get out of bed, others more fortunate to linger yet another half hour before venturing the icy kitchens, Lijah's candle gave a bright flickering light through the gloom. He had risen from his curtainless, featherless bed and was busying himself around his cottage, lighting the sticks he had gathered from the hedge bottom to kindle a little fire for his and Jane's humble morning breakfast. What a defiant air he has as after breakfast he directs his footsteps through the grey light of morning. His whole being makes no secret of the severity of his day's work ahead. Beneath that slouched broadbrimmed hat, green with age and storm-stained, his face still rosy, his mouth showing gaps in his teeth, there is, this morning, a toil worn look in his features. He wears a smock over his coarse, patched under-garments; his gaiters partly cover his blue stockings and his heavy, hobnailed boots complete his working attire. His frail basket is slung from his shoulder by a leather strap with his hunk of bread and cheese tied in a red and white spotted kerchief inside. He takes no drink; George Hedgecock or Anne will send a costrel barrel of cider for him by one of the servant girls—more than he is allowed for ploughing on account of the thirst he will get as the flail beats dust from the wheat sheaves.

It is early, but George Hedgecock yawns as he sits up in bed. Then Harry Steel, lantern in hand, meets Lijah in the yard as he ties up the milking cows. The cock crows, Harry's dog barks; the disturbed carrion crow caws from the leafless elm, the fresh calved cow moos and is answered by her offspring from the calf pen, the horses are whinnying for their hay (George will feed them later). Then, as Harry douts his lantern, a quarter circle of the bright red sun peeps boldly over Stanway Hill, in minutes the full circle can be seen. It's daytime in Winter at Ayshon.

No other villager meets Lijah at Sundial to pass the time of day, but as he pulls the wooden peg from asp and staple of the great barn doors, doors big enough to allow a loaded waggon to enter, he is followed. There is a great stir in the farmyard. Like a pack of hungry hounds, all the animals loose in the Winter fold follow Lijah to gorge at the troughs of food. The straw-fed cattle, the market pony, yearling colts, all jockey for positions to pull at the hay racks.

The pigeons glide down from the nearby cote to search the chaff for a grain or two; the poultry stand cautiously under the lintel as Lijah throws off his top clothes, worn and patched in places—worn by time and toil, Winter and rough weather. Rolling up the sleeves of his rough hairy shirt, he exposes to the gathering light a pair of stalwart arms—arms still brown from the harvest sun, wrists pliable as withies, hands horny and calloused by shuppick and rake. Lijah pauses a minute while he sizes up the situation in the Long Barn. He then walks slowly to the threshing floor, gathers a skip full of shed grain and chaff which he scatters outside the barn doors for the following hens, cocks and geese. The double barn doors are in fact four doors; the top half opens independently of the bottom, so Lijah closes the poultry out by shutting the bottom doors—the top ones let in the daylight. The other stock are shut off from the threshing section of the barn by a gate at the end of the hay rack.

Lijah thinks to himself, "Now I'm in my prison among the sheaves." The cob-webbed roof, stalls of wattle and daub, were carried by great beams of whole trees, shaped by the adze, marked in numbers and signs at the joints by the carpenters of a couple of hundred years ago. The east and west gabled ends were in Cotswold stone off Bredon Hill, rough hewn but laid in courses with smooth corner quoins. These ends provided the only windows, if windows they can be called. It was as if the builder had intended to make the barn lighter by leaving on the inside open slats eighteen inches wide, two feet six inches high, then, as course of stone was laid on course, the window lights were drawn in towards the outside of the wall at an acute angle so that the light penetrated a six inch slit. The place gave the appearance of a fortification with peepholes through. Lijah took no notice of this. "Always bin the same," he had been told. A boarded partition near the threshing floor formed a cub to rake or shove the unwinnowed grain into after the threshing. I suppose many people would think that a man destined to such toil closed his mind to the outside world so that all his strength would be used swinging the flail. This was not true in the case of Lijah Hicks. Many Winters he had gripped the same hand staff, a slender stick, five feet of ash, but he had broken or worn out many swingels of knotty crab apple or holly. This was life as it had been for centuries.

He started by threshing the red-bearded wheat, cutting each sheaf bond with his knife. He knew of old that the red-bearded wheat was loath to part from the chaff so it was with all the power he possessed that his flail was borne down onto the ears. Other wheat, where the chaff was half open like beechmast, didn't need quite the threshing the red-bearded did. George Hedgecock needed the straw for thatching some of his buildings, so when Lijah had beaten the grain and chaff from several sheaves, he laid a bond of straw across the floor and tied the threshed straw into tidy boltings. The red grain and chaff were swept into the cub.

He had been threshing a little while this Winter morning when one of Hedgecock's servant girls came with his cider. Stopping a while, he poured a horn out of the costrel barrel, took a sip, wiped his brow and watched the sunbeams make magic with the dust as the sun peeped through the slit windows. Pretty, he thought, not like the rainbow though as comes when I'm in the fields singing behind the plough. The girl disturbed two wood pigeons perched in the pear tree near the door. Their wings clapped as they joined the fowls scratching for the last of the corn and chaff. It will be a long and lonely Winter here, Lijah thought as he longed to be out in the open, regardless of the wind and weather. Ah, to hear the cry of the peewit, the chatter of the starlings under the trees as they fought for the fallen crab apples, to see the leafless hedges with their late harvest of haws, hips and sloes. But Lijah thought again as his hard stick parted the golden grain from its cocoon of chaff.

As a robin ventured into the barn, hopping from the doorway, then perching on the top rail of the dividing gate, Lijah realised that the little red-breasted bird had become both hungry and tame. How brave he flits about the woodland trees when the sun is overhead, the Summer showers providing enough and to spare for his food. Now, in Winter, he becomes a bird only seen in garden, rickyard, and where men live, but doesn't he bring a brightness to the Winter scene. The fields, Lijah thought, have their beauty, their charm, to the farmer; the flocks and herds to the grazier.

Lijah laid down his flail for a few minutes while he ate his bread and a little cheese and drank deeply from his gallon of cider. Sitting down on a bolting of straw, he let his mind roam through the seasons. How he ploughed the virgin turf, sowed the seed, cut the thistles, gathered the hay. 'Tis a fine job working among the scented dried herbage. He thought of the sweat, the salty sweat, how it made his eyes smart; how the midday sun beat down, how the hayseeds showered down his shirt as he roped the loads of hay. Healthy life, he thought, different from the dusty barn. As he rose from his bolting seat, flurries of snow swept by, the winds fell in all directions as the farm buildings parted the drift as a breakwater parts the sea. Lijah went on threshing. Darkness fell so gradually that evening that long after the hens had gone to the roosts George Hedgecock from his kitchen could still hear the whack, whack, whack of Lijah's flail. At long last, when the barn became too dark to work in, the owls started their nightly patrol for food, pheasants in the wood began their Cock up, Cock up leaving no secret as to where their nightly perch was, Lijah laid down his flail, slipped on his smock frock and picked up his basket. The hobnails of his boots made sparks in the growing darkness when, bent and tired, he slouched down the cobbled slope, through the roadside gate, then across the road to his cottage, where, by the fireside, he had some talk— almost the first since early morning— with Jane who told him how quiet the day had been apart from the distant whack, whack of his flail.

Hedgecocks the Yeomen

As the nineteenth century dawned on Ayshon and Broddy Tower became a familiar sight, so the Hedgecocks increased their hold on Bredon Hill acres. Mark had married Elizabeth Stokes and took over Ayshon Wood on the death of the old Methodist, Jonah Stubbs. Harry Steel and Lijah Hicks still worked at Sundial Farm, now run by Andrew Hedgecock, George having part-retired with Anne to The Glen, a half-timbered house and orchard up Holcomb Lane. Mathilda Trusswell had left the village with Gregory after he had become Colonel Trusswell and finished his time in the army.

"He ant let her stop empty long," Lijah told the new young landlord at the Plough, Harry Vale. "Thirteen youngsters her av had to my knowledge— that don't include them as her a slipped. Still, they be amus growed up; some be in the Navy, some in the Church, and they do say, Harry, that stock's as good as money. 'Twas sad about Proctor Perkins, his missus and youngsters a

Tree trunk and tree tops.

Parkland — ''The foresight of our fathers and forefathers in planting the trees.''

going off with the smallpox.'' Steve Bostock had been another victim of the outbreak.

"I wonder, and yet I don't,''—old Job Allen coughed as the tart cider caught his breath when he swallowed—"who will have Bostock's farm now he lies anant the beech tree in the churchyard? It's up to Sir John and Lady Franklin, unt it?''

Harold Holmes, the squire's carter, who still remained single, said, "But you knows, Jobey, it ull be the Hedgecocks. Young Andrew who took over from his dad 'ull have Bostock's place and take on old Fred Pickford, for what he's worth at seventy-five, and Dick Hicks.''

The year 1800 progressed from New Year to Candlemas, Candlemas to Shrove Tuesday, then through Lent to Easter—the ploughing, the working of the ground and the sowing.

Richard Surman and Catherine had raised two fine daughters. Phil Besford, who had farmed Highford House, retired with his aged housekeeper to Woodbine Cottage; the land, with Abel Smith still active at the plough tails, was taken over by landlord and Squire Franklin. This was a year of immense change in Ayshon and Beckford. Lord and Lady Waterford were not happy to see the end of the cottage farmers—the part-time men—and he and his good lady were not sorry to leave the country scene. Both died the same week and Jack Baker buried them in the sand and gravel of Beckford with all the pomp and ceremony of Bishop and robed clergy.

Jim Bradfield was one of the few who understood enclosure from a cottage farmer's point of view. "Ah,'' he sighed. "We've lost our champion. His Lordship never wanted Ayshon and Beckford to be farmed by big men; he studied the likes a we. You would still have your ridge of land and your pig, Job, if Waterford hadn't a bin ruled by Trusswell and Franklin.''

"That's as may be,'' Job Allen replied as they stood together by the old Squire's grave. "But if only the Government will peg the price of corn, we shan't be too badly off. Rabbits be got so plentiful on Bredon Hill that Sir John Franklin, just back from London, says as they told him there that one of the London cries of the street hawkers be Bredon Hill Rabbits. They goes up on the Worcester–London stage coach."

Now that Bernard Baker had passed on at Ayshon, Jim Bradfield alone was left to tell the tale of the days of the strips, the days of the Common, the days of no work, the days at the plough, the times before six days were worked for squire and yeoman. "Hedgecocks were got big farmers" was everyone's opinion in Ayshon. No one was jealous of their success; they had worked and planned themselves into that position of relative comfort. But Andrew Hedgecock at twenty-seven was still unmarried, although Moses Steel who worked for him had already started a family at the Cross Cottage — two boys and a girl.

After harvest at Sundial Farm, Andrew put his men to their tasks of threshing, the flail ringing in every Hedgecock barn. Old Harry Steel and Lijah still made the cider, fed the stock in the home yard. Andrew grew restless of the ordinary humdrum life of the village. The golden guineas from the harvest, from the sale of black cart horses at Stow, from the sale of lambs, of butter and cheese, grew into larger piles at Sundial. Mark plodded along with his small farm in the wood. Andrew, besides managing Sundial for his father, found time to hunt and shoot and to gamble at Worcester cockpit, but he had none for women. "Why should I keep another man's daughter?" he said. He grew reckless at cards and George Hedgecock, who still held the reins at Sundial and still paid the rent, brought in Mark to keep the place as it had always been — a clean tidy farm with stock and crops looking kind.

Then one day in November, Andrew left word with Tom Steel

that he was off to London. Tom was ordered to drive him to
Pershore in the light cart pulled by one of the strong cobs. There
Andrew caught the Worcester to London stage coach, dressed as
a typical West Country yeoman. In London he met some of the
doubtful characters who visited the Worcester cockpit; he wined
and dined, gambled with cards and dice; visited Tyburn to see the
executions; went bear baiting; spent many nights at balls and
theatres; made love to merchants' daughters, to officers'
daughters, to daughters of no one, and then it happened—he fell
in love with a London wine merchant's daughter he met at a ball. He
made love to her nightly and she returned his love; he, as Lijah
Hicks would have said, "colted her". Realising her position, she
eloped with him—a flaxen haired beauty she was of twenty
summers. As the London coach neared Pershore, Tom Steel,
following his orders, was waiting to meet it. Back at Sundial
Farm, the servants were ready with a hot meal to welcome the
return of Andrew and his bride to be. Andrew's housekeeper
arranged for her bedroom to be in the south wing of the farm
house, Andrew slept under the Sundial over the front porch.
As Lijah said to Harry, "It's no good locking the stable door
when the horse as bolted; there's no doubt they lay anant of
one another up in London, 'tis only natur, unt it."

The following Spring it was evident that Barbara Mellor, the
wine merchant's daughter, was not putting on weight just on
account of Andrew's housekeeper's cooking.

"Not just the fat bacon, is it, Dad?" Tom Hicks said to
Lijah.

"Nor the new bread," Lijah answered. "Her a got a young
Hedgecock under ur petticoat or else my eyesight is hellishly
poor." The wise men, the talkers and the shocked women were
all right—Barbara was in the family way.

Then the news got to Richard Surman, who had been asked to

marry them at St Andrew's Church. Surman was a tolerant man, a man to see the best in his flock, but Andrew's adventures in London displeased him, especially as Andrew was his brother-in-law. Andrew, the cuckoo lamb, had started off on the wrong foot. "It's unavoidable among the labouring classes with their hovels overcrowded; this encourages them to drink and to lust. But you, Andrew, you went to my school, your father is an upright man, my churchwarden."

"To hell with you, Richard, and St Andrew's—I wish to God you hadn't given me that name. I'm a stockbreeder."

"I can't see what difference that makes, that's no excuse for fornication."

"Well, look here," said Andrew. "Come down and have a glass and a pipe tonight and I'll try to explain, man to man. This won't be in front of Barbara either, nor you won't divulge anything to Catherine."

"Fair enough, Andrew," said Richard Surman. "I will come down and give you a fair hearing. I'm a shepherd, Andrew, but my flock don't often go as far as London. Tonight then."

At Sundial Farm that night Andrew and Richard faced each other, one each side of the log fire, the candles on the sideboard flickering in the draught. A young servant girl brought in the sherry, together with a wicker basket of long clay pipes, and the tobacco jar. When their pipes were nicely going and the two men lounged back in their chairs, Andrew spoke first.

"Have a drink, Richard, it's supposed to be a good vintage. Barbara's father's a wine merchant, I've learnt a lot in London."

"No doubt, Andrew, that's what I'm here for—to hear your story."

Andrew puffed thoughtfully at his pipe, cleared his throat and began. "You say you are a shepherd, Richard. That's as may be, I earn my living from stockbreeding like my father did. Now many's the time I've gone to Tewkesbury market along with Dad to buy bulling heifers, that's young female cattle ready for the bull. It's no good buying cattle that won't breed, it's a gamble buying bulling heifers, it's best to buy those already in calf. It's the same at Stow, you can buy fillies or young mares there fit to go to the stallion, but what if they won't breed? It's safer to buy one already stinted—one in foal."

"What are you getting at, Andrew?"

"Just this, Richard; a farmer worth his salt doesn't marry a girl till she's proven, that's until he knows whether she will bear a family. It's not the looks a farmer goes by, it's her ability to breed, to turn the butter churn—he wants a strong, fertile lass. I know it's comparing women with animals a bit but I'm talking man to man and Barbara has proved herself. She is in the family way and what's more she has proved herself in another way."

Richard Surman had had many heart to heart talks with his parishioners but none quite like this.

"Andrew," he said, "at least I can see your logic up to a point, but aren't you making use of Barbara?—not being quite fair. How about if you gave her up, wouldn't that be bad for her?"

"Give her up?" Andrew said as he poked the log fire making the sparks fly up the open chimney between the two inglenooks. "Not likely. She's got everything, God never made such a beautiful creature before."

"What else has she got?" Richard enquired, adding, "I've married some gems at Ayshon Church."

"Well, it's like this." Andrew was loath to talk to his brother-in-law in such businesslike, matter of fact terms, then he blurted out, "muscles".

"Muscles," repeated Rev. Surman. "You want a wife, not a weight lifter."

"Both," said Andrew as his right hand automatically touched his shoulder, then shot straight out towards Richard. As his muscles tensed and flexed Richard noticed an artful twinkle in his brother-in-law's eye. Andrew explained how he had taken Barbara to St Andrew's church and got her to lift the lid of the heavy chest in the vestry. "She lifted it as if it were a feather. You have been in charge of St Andrew's for many years, Richard, didn't you know that farmers in these parts try out their prospective wives this way?"

Surman left Sundial Farm that night a somewhat puzzled man, but he arranged to marry Andrew and Barbara when the banns had been called.

"Don't leave it any longer," he begged Andrew. "It's becoming very evident now that another Hedgecock will soon be here."

George and Anne liked Barbara. George thought his son had made a good choice as a bed mate, to cook and to help in the dairy. Not that the last two duties would matter for long; Andrew was fast becoming prosperous enough to employ village girls in the kitchen and dairy. So Andrew married Barbara at St Andrew's in the Spring of 1801, the very year the first census was made, and her name went on it as Andrew's wife of Sundial Farm. Jim Bradfield said that it was a pity the census wasn't the year before.

"We av lost a few over the Winter," he said. "Old uns like Bernard Baker."

"But it was unwise to count heads when Napoleon had thousands at Boulogne waiting to invade the country," Richard Surman told the folk at church.

CHAPTER SEVEN

Hearts of Oak

The Press Gang, 1802

EARLY IN 1801 Andrew Hedgecock's wife, Barbara, gave birth to Horatio Hedgecock, named after the great Horatio Nelson who had shaken Napoleon's forces at the Battle of the Nile in 1798. In the summer of that year, Archdeacon Trusswell preached his last sermon at Beckford church. He implored able-bodied young men to join the forces and save Britain from Bonaparte's plan to invade England.

Sir John Franklin spared some of his younger men for the forces. In some ways the men were better off serving under the Crown. At least they had food and drink, clothing and shelter. A succession of bad harvests was one of the causes of soaring prices; wheaten bread, which at Ayshon a few years before was sixpence a loaf, rose to one shilling and fivepence. Some villages, where the price of bread determined the wages of the labourers, fared better, but the situation in Ayshon was one of increasing parish relief for the labouring classes who lived mainly on bread, potatoes and turnips. Meat at sevenpence a pound became a luxury.

In his last weeks on earth, the old Archdeacon softened his outlook. He knew full well that at any time now he would leave Beckford. He was a rich man and Gregory, his nephew, was well provided for, so he called Richard Surman over from Ayshon and as a final gesture to the two villages under the hill—villages he had not always treated fairly—he left in his will a sum of money for charity, the interest to buy bread for the poor of the parishes. He died at a ripe old age and, like Stephen in the Bible, was carried to his burial by devout men: Norman Bosley, Tom Steel, Dick Hicks and Andrew Stokes. It was the Archdeacon's wish that the Reverend Richard Surman, who had laboured so many years under him, should do the duty at Beckford church that day. Lord Coventry's son, George, came over from Croome Court. The Hedgecocks attended in full strength. The two villages mourned a man who had upheld the established church, but in fact they mourned more from a sense of duty than one of loss. Loss it was to the ruling classes of the parishes, but to the poor he had only relented at the eleventh hour.

In the Plough at Ayshon, Harry and Sue Vale brewed good beer, sold excellent cider and Malvern Hill Perry, and in every way proved good successors to Proctor Perkins.

"Boney's amassing troops across the Channel," Tom Steel told the company there one evening. "Surman gets the papers from Worcester by carrier and they says there's 130,000 men a-laying in wait with flat-bottomed boats, and Napoleon boasts that if he can rule the Straits of Dover for six hours, he can invade England."

Norman Bosley was over from Beckford. He was now head shepherd for Sir John Franklin— Sir John who had become the new Lord Waterford on the death of his father— and it was Norman who had taken the late Bernard Baker's inglenook seat. He looked thoughtfully into the fire.

"Rev. Surman may read the papers, but the new vicar, though not such a man of letters as the Archdeacon, studies the politics of the great powers and he reckons that Nelson's fleet ull scatter the French before very long."

Old Jim Bradfield spoke up then. "If it unt religion, it's politics in this house. I wish to God somebody ud talk about the harvest and the hay crop for a change."

Tom Steel leaned against the dresser, picked up a pewter tankard and asked Sue Vale to fill it with perry. As he supped the real Malvern Hill stuff, he explained to Jim quite kindly how we stood against the French. "If he turns his great army westward towards us we shall be under his heel. The gentry will be guillotined same as the noblemen of France. I'm telling you, although we be eighty miles from the sea, Boney a got his eye on this county of ours."

Jim sniffed, lighting his short clay pipe from Harry Vale's embers. "Hast ever sin the channel at Dover, any on ya?"

One old sweat who had sailed in the slave ships bringing sugar from the Indies said he had and added, "The French Navy will never outwit Nelson."

Then Jim Bradfield recollected a threat of invasion long ago. "Not many left in Ayshon now," he said, "can remember the '45 when the Pretender invaded England with his Scottish Highlanders. The English treated it as a joke, five thousand men trying to occupy the country and put King George off the throne. Of course he was banking on the English joining forces with him on the way south. Durby was as far as he got, just past Brumigum. Bonnie Prince Charlie, a fine looking fellow, went back to Scotland tail between his legs. I beunt afraid of no invader."

As the talk got livelier in Vale's kitchen, Dick Hicks came rushing in and asked Harry Vale for a quart as quick as he could draw one. "Startling news down the Severn," he said. "The Press Gang be out. Fishermen, as you all knows, beunt taken for the Army but they wants um in the Navy."

"What of that?" Tom Steel said as he nearly straightened his back under one of the low beams across the Plough ceiling. "They don't want the likes a we for the Navy, we be producing the fittle, growing the corn, rearing the cattle, the lambs, the pigs. That's our effort agin Boney."

Although the customers of the Plough slept soundly in their beds that night, they remembered next morning Dick's words about the Press Gang. Days passed in Ayshon, Lijah Hicks, helped by his son Dick, bred from Hedgecock's mares the black horses of the Midlands: five years on the land, then to the cities. But more and more were bought by the Army to pull the guns and supplies awaiting invasion.

June 26th came round, the day of the Pershore Fair, when haymaking traditionally began in the brook meadows. Scythes laid low the grass, buttercups and other flowers of the field, the ring of whetstone on blade became familiar once more in Ayshon. The Ayshon men took to using scythes as ducks take to water. The mown grass in the swathe showed up plainly the shape of the fields— fields fenced at the Enclosure, irregularly patterned fields with fences following the contour of the land, the course of a water ditch, a line of old trees. Clockwise the mowers moved with a rhythm not unlike that of dancers on the polished ballroom floor. Backs slightly bent, the scythe blade never left the cool damp ground as deep semicircles ate their way into the standing ley. Silently this age-old annual slaughter of fetch, coltsfoot, timothy vetch, buttercup, cowslip and clover made pollen showers drift in the breeze, field mice scurry from their nests, and partridge and plover leave at the last minute their clutches of eggs. Silently, yes, until the scythe blade shaving the ground ran into an occasional mole heave; then the newly turned earth which the mole had thrown up into little hillocks clogged the sweeping blade bringing forth the usual damn and blast from the mower as, scythe on end with blade shoulder-high, he cleaned the tool of the sticky earth with bare hands.

George Hedgecock had told Andrew to take on young Adam Bosley, Norman's son, as an extra hand on the ever growing Sundial Farm. Adam, a stripling fellow not afraid of work, brought up by Norman and his wife among the sheep on Bredon Hill, lived in a cottage by the quarry which was known as Cobblers. Adam could follow the plough tails, sow the corn and use the shears, and that very haymaking Norman taught him how to use the scythe.

George Hedgecock rode around the hill one July morning with young Andrew. He rode on his weight-carrying hunter; he needed a good horse under him, for his weight had increased with age. Andrew, a slim, athletic type of fellow, rode a filly with a lot of breeding in her—one he raced at local meetings.

"Tomorrow, Andrew," his father said, "we'll mow Church Close."

"But the men are busy carrying the brook meadows," Andrew answered as their horses took them, side by side, on the bridle path from Sundial Farm to the church.

"We can spare Adam Bosley and Lijah Hicks."

"But Lijah, Dad? He loads the waggons from the pitchers."

George Hedgecock pulled up his horse under an ancient oak, its fresh leaves giving shade from the summer sun for horse and rider.

"Lijah Hicks is no longer safe on load nor rick, and see to it, my lad, that he never builds either again." George went on, "Lijah has worked for me many long years, you see. I've shared so many good and bad harvests with him. When he weaves his way up Ayshon Street now, it's not always the cider he's had; his legs have got too weak to carry that belly of his, and then on hot sunny days he's apt to go swimmy in the head—giddy if you like. I've studied Lijah—he's safer with both feet on the ground. I've had the best out of him and shouldn't like anything to happen to him now."

As the brook meadows were cleared by the pitchers and loaders, Ayshon's young women following behind with their heel rakes, Adam Bosley would dearly have liked to share his bread and cheese and cider with Mary, Andrew's new dairy maid. Mary had come from Wales, and as she sang her Welsh songs, the

hearts of the men also made music. To them she was another
Ruth, another gleaner. But Mary was raking the fallen hay for the
pitchers now, and as she worked she sang, a pretty picture with
her hat awry, the bloom of youth on her smiling face. The July
heat caused the men to strip to their shirts—their smocks hung
drying from sweat on the hawthorn. Mary threw off her gown
showing her stout brown leather stays—what a hindrance these
were for work, why were they so high? Eagerly Dick Hicks and
Tom Steel, Hedgecock's hay pitchers, glanced over their forkfuls
of hay to see revealed to their sight Mary's bare lily-white neck,
her full ripe bosom, even whiter still, exposed for the first time
this year to the warm sun's rays. What jokes Dick and Tom
exchanged on their short journeys from the waggon to the haycocks! Then she stopped a moment to speak in her lilting Welsh
accent and stroke back the ringlets from her glowing cheeks. As
the hooped keg of home brewed ale, that thirst-laxing cordial,
was uncorked beneath the withies in the cool of the brook, the
men pressed the friendly horn, prized as a goblet, into Mary's
hand. Said Dick to Tom as she drank, never had a nicer pair of
lips ever pressed against the drinking horn.

"Heavy work for a girl like you, Mary," Tom said to her, as
quietly and politely as he could, as if he were talking to a
goddess of the hayfields, and wiping his brow he passed the horn
to Dick.

"Oh no," she said. "Not as hard as churning the butter,
especially when it just won't come—the curd, I mean," and
grabbing her rake again she went to work gathering up every
stray wisp of hay, her sweet shrill voice singing some Welsh air
unknown and unheard of in Ayshon. As she sang and she raked,
music filled the brookside meadows; when she stopped, nothing
was heard but the creaking of her stays.

Next morning, Lijah and Adam Bosley carried their scythes

and whetstones, their frail baskets of food, their costrel barrels of home brewed beer, up through the pathway among the gravestones at St Andrew's church into the Close. Lijah led the way as the old and new mowers circled the field, Adam close behind him. Andrew Hedgecock rode from Sundial soon after the milking was finished and placed two nut sticks in the unmown hay where he knew a pheasant and a partridge were sitting. "Leave a tussock around the nest, Lijah." Lijah nodded, going on with his mowing as the grass, still wet with dew, fell before his scythe.

As he and Adam drew near to the Monk's fishpond and were whetting their scythes with their whetstones, two strange-looking men came through the churchyard.

"They beunt natives of Bredon Hill," Lijah observed. "They looks like the Military. A party of them were in Ayshon village from down the Severn Vale with two fishermen they had picked up below Tewkesbury. The Press Gang they be. I'll talk to um," Lijah whispered.

"Young fella," they addressed Adam. "We want you to come with us to fight in King George's Navy. Drop that scythe, look sharp!"

Lijah's old eyes met theirs man to man as they stood. "Leave that bwoy to me, kip your distance if you want two legs left to go back with."

"You impudent old sod," their leader exclaimed, "to defy his Majesty's men."

"Cut um just below the knee, Adam. Thy scythe ull tackle that leg now 'ee have had the whetstone on him."

If they had been drilled for this action, drilled for months on the barrack square, Lijah and Adam could not have dealt better with the intruders. As Lijah took a few sweeps with his scythe towards the legs of the Press Gang, the point missing their calves by a mere hand's breadth, Adam with every sinew tensed swung hard and shoulder high at the gang.

"This field has got to be mown by sunset tomorrow, so to hell with you lot and leave Adam and me to do it."

"You defy me when I say that that young fella's coming with us?" the leader said.

"See that churchyard yonder? Many good Ayshon men be there, so stand back or else you will be lying with um and we don't like the likes a you alongside God-fearing Ayshon men."

"Hold your scythes! You know Nelson wants men for his Navy and that fella will suit us very well."

With a final warning from Lijah, the gang stood by the pond. "Now, Adam," he said, "Charge!"

The old sweat and the young recruit, with scythes shining in the afternoon sun, made for the gang. They turned tail and ran down St Andrew's churchyard only to be met by George Hedgecock who had watched and listened to it all from under the yew tree. George laughed at Lijah's effrontery, praised Adam's courage; haymaking went on in Ayshon but Admiral Nelson had to manage without Adam Bosley.

George Hedgecock smoked a pipe after an evening meal with his son-in-law Richard Surman. The meal had been in the true Hedgecock tradition, supervised by both Anne Hedgecock, who remained active despite her years, and her daughter Catherine. The leg of lamb, the peas, the potatoes were all home grown. Harry Steel had imparted his skill in killing and dressing lambs to his son Tom. Often the milk lambs straight from their mother were bought by the butchers, but most weekends during the Summer when the July sun, the grass, the wild thyme and clover on Bredon Hill had imparted that extra flavour to the lamb, Tom killed and dressed one for George Hedgecock and family. The white milk-fed meat off the spit was so tender that it melted in

The Press Gang—"Nelson wants men for his Navy."

Invasion of England. "A view of the French raft, as seen afloat at St. Maloes, in February 1798. This machine is 600 feet long and 300 broad, mounts 500 pieces of cannon, 36 and

the mouth, so different from the darker meat of the winter teg. The gooseberry pie and cream, the wine, in their own way had been as excellent.

Richard Surman, who studied the papers and politics of Europe and America, agreed with his father-in-law that the retention of Adam Bosley from serving in Nelson's fleet was right.

"If your harvest is spoilt and others with it, the price of food will soar higher and higher," he pointed out. "The Press Gang will no doubt pick up idlers and take them to Bristol. Adam Bosley's heart and soul is in the land. His place is at Sundial Farm. I can think of other men in the parish whose absence would hardly be noticed, but no one could say that of Adam Bosley."

Hunting, Shooting and William Havelock

When William Havelock came to Beckford vicarage in 1803 at the age of twenty-seven, he was still a bachelor. His first love was the church. But he was a man stirred by the chase. He kept a few hounds to course hares on Bredon Hill, keeping himself fit by exercise. Soon he found a friend in the great landowner at Croome Court. Lord and Lady Coventry and George had increased their packs of foxhounds; they had kennels at Croome and some at Broddy. His Lordship's huntsmen, his grooms, his whippers and his strappers all found full employment with the hunt. They hunted the Avon and Severn Vale, or shall we say that part of the Severn near its junction with the Avon; they hunted Bredon Hill, Broddy Hill, the North Cotswolds.

Gilbert White wrote in his *Natural History of Selborne*: "If the stationary man would pay some attention to the district in which he resides and publish his thoughts respecting the objects that surround him, from such material might be drawn the most complete county history.'' The Rev. William Havelock was such a man, a man who lived very near to nature itself. He recognised the old love of sport discoverable in his ancestors and inherited from generation to generation; he was a link connecting past generations with the present. It didn't really matter to the natives of Ayshon whether they indulged in sport or not. What meant a great deal was their willingness to recall olden times, memories of pluck and daring, to enjoy rough and ready tales or the melody of some old song sung by an aged man of Ayshon. George Hedgecock in his old age still rode to hounds and meets at the Plough were a chance for him to show his hospitality to followers from the Bredon Hill country.

Richard Surman loved the country as it was. He loved the fields, the hills, flowers, trees, birds and beasts; he was not a man of the chase. Young William Havelock told Richard that although they might differ in their views of hunting, he must admit that such sport did help to relieve the monotony of country life. But for the horses and hounds and the opportunities they gave for neighbours to meet, to talk farming, to talk of almost anything, the life of a country gentleman would be duller. Lord Coventry was pleased that the new vicar of Beckford was a hunting man and a shooting man. To his mind Surman was soft-hearted about the stag, the hare, the fox, liking to see and hear them in the woods and fields.

Lord Coventry invited Havelock over to Croome Court for a few days to show him over his estates.

''The woods yonder,'' he said, ''were planted by my father—grand old woods they are, a delight to the eye. What a calamity if they were lost! Planted, mark you, for bird and beast, but at regular intervals for the wily fox to break cover and the hounds to make music as they chase him, running with the wind to deaden his scent, then perhaps going to ground in some unstopped earth.''

Some days he and Havelock rode along the Avon Vale where the willows hid the river as it snaked its way around Bredon Hill. Some days they rode to Broddy Hill and, after a visit to the kennels, up the steep slopes to the Folly. Havelock was no stranger to country life but looking down on the vale below Broddy Tower made a great impression on him. ''Those green fertile fields are a grand sight, sir; indeed they almost laugh. The signs of a plentiful harvest show clearly from this vantage point. Human industry, man's work in God's world, is pleasing to the eye.''

''Ah yes,'' Lord Coventry replied. ''It's a pretty sight from here, but my tenants are ploughing another furrow or two nearer the hedge each year. These are hungry years, Vicar. It means that now the bluebells and violets, foxgloves and primroses are being driven from the hedgerows more each year. Fox covers are plentiful among the wild flowers, safe from ploughshare and spade; it's a comforting thought that there nature takes its yearly course. Then there are the waste lands on these wolds where the song of the birds and the sound of the breeze can be enjoyed uninterrupted by man and machine.''

As the two rode side by side over the hills, Havelock remarked on Charles Wesley's hymn, ''Give me the faith that can remove, and sink the mountain to a plain.''

''Good men, the Wesley brothers,'' his Lordship replied. ''Thousands of miles in the saddle John Wesley did on his preaching tours, and we have a lot to thank the Almighty for, William, as we are riding here. How the workers pent up in a city factory or at a shop counter must long for the fields, for a breath of fresh air, to see and hear the lark on the wing in the sunshine. The birds sing their songs by the rides as finely as any choir; their song

peals through the cathedral of the woods. Our labourers in the
fields have a hard life in Winter, but in the Spring, like you and
me, they see miracles happen every day and their lot is better.
What is it regenerates the clods in the valley into life, clothes
seemingly dead twigs in green and trees in blossom? The sap
rises, the warmer winds blow and it seems that all the mechanism
of nature is in motion. Does anyone doubt that as April comes to
an end, the first note of the cuckoo will be heard, that the may
will bloom over the smithy door and waggoners pick it to
bedeck their horses' bridles?''

Lord Coventry and Havelock agreed that to lose our woods
would be to lose the Spring and Summer haunts of our migrating
birds. Their preservation had depended on the foresight of our
fathers and grandfathers in planting the trees.

"Richard Surman's a good man at Ayshon," Lord Coventry
said as the two riders rode across the vale to Bredon Hill. "He's
entitled to his opinion about hunting and the like, and he keeps
his thoughts to himself."

At that moment a woodpecker laughed from a nearby copse;
the blackbirds too were in full song.

"To lose that," Lord Coventry said, "and the song of the
thrush, the woodlark, the nightingale . . . it's not to be thought
of."

Spring turned to Summer, Summer to harvest. The partridge
and landrail ran in front of the men who cut the corn by hook
and by crook. The sharp blade of the bagging hook, the wooden
pickthank helped to make the music of harvest. Havelock harvested his glebe, shot partridge, coursed hares, preached at
Beckford each Sunday. His staff at the vicarage was ample for a
young single man: a good homely housekeeper, maids, gardeners,
grooms and a couple of farm labourers. He looked forward to the
fox-hunting season as a bride looks forward to her wedding.

Lord Coventry made Lord Waterford Master of the Foxhounds. Huntsmen in pink, whippers-in and strappers surrounded the thatched Red Lion at Beckford for the opening meet. Havelock rode hard and fearless as the hounds found their fox in Beckford coppice. The baying of their leaders, the sound of the huntsman's horn broke the stillness of that misty November morning. Andrew Hedgecock and Peter Trusswell were among the followers from Ayshon. Francis Stokes, Waterford's bailiff, rode a heavy hunter. He wore the breeches, gaiters and box hat typical of a man of his station. Norman Bosley had been up before daylight earth-stopping on Bredon Hill, Tom Steel had stopped the fox earths on Elmley Castle side. Reynard made for Ayshon Wood where Dick Hicks was working. As he approached the larches through the fern, bracken and blackberry bushes, Dick gave the *View halloo* as loud as he could shout. The pack followed a knee high scent through the wood towards Elmley Castle where, in a stubble field, they bowled him over. He had given them a good run for the first meet of the season. It was unusual for an old stager to be caught so soon after the cubs were fit for a good run, but an old stager he was. William Havelock, being the first horseman at the Hill, claimed his grey brush. Barbara Hedgecock was close on his heels, so the vicar presented her with the fox tail.

Lord Coventry had now reached an age when one day a week with the foxhounds was enough for him, but he relied on his huntsmen and his son George to provide his many friends with the sport of the chase.

Havelock had hunted with the Coventry pack further up the Severn Valley before he came to Beckford. He knew George Priddey, the squire's whipper. George spoke of the country he knew fifty miles around Croome, with a four o'clock breakfast of underdone beef, eggs and brandy. He and Phoebe Hunt, his mistress (George followed the gentry in such diversions) could top a flight of rails, skim ridge and furrow, charge a fence. Phoebe, a perfect Diana, egged him on to take hazardous leaps. George in turn wagered that Phoebe would leap against any woman in England. With Phoebe and Priddey on the scent, there was no telling where the pack might be called off their fox. It was said that once they penetrated deep into the Radnor Forest, hearing the hounds in full cry; Priddey vowed he would follow the fox like a devil to the doors of hell.

The Beckford vicar, Andrew Hedgecock, George Coventry and Lord Waterford were, with Mark Hedgecock, all hunting mad. On a winter afternoon, after dining at three o'clock, they left Beckford Hall to draw the coppice as dusk approached.

"It's a moonlight night," Priddey said as he led a dozen couple of hounds up Bredon Hill. The "Hark-in" was given. Old Pilot, an experienced leading hound, took turns in and out of the spinney, lashing with his stern. "Have at him!" shouted Priddey.

"Get ready," Lord Waterford ordered from his position astride his hunter.

The moon shone clear over the vale.

"Hold hard," shouted Andrew.

Then a "Tally-ho" from William Havelock. With every hound out of cover, sterns up, a breast-high scent, horses in line, as straight as a gun barrel, reynard made for the tongue of the next coppice, then to the Firs and away to Bredon summit to give horses, riders and hounds a midnight airing. Running into the moonlight, Priddey called "Gone away" on the horn. The hounds gathered around the Old Soul, Priddey's horse, and the small field moved off home to spend the rest of the night at the Hall. Lord Waterford's staff had provided a meal of well-hung game, shot and hawked by none other than the Rev. William Havelock. After they had both drunk of the frothy juice of the hop, Lord Waterford chivvied the vicar by reciting these lines:

> A parson once had a remarkable foible,
> Of loving good liquor far more than his bible.
> His neighbours all said he was much less perplexed
> In handling a tankard than handling a text.

After some ums and ahs, Havelock retorted, "What about Dryden's squire? Here's his verse:

> 'The first physicians by debauch were made,
> Excess began, and sloth sustains the trade.
> By chase, our long lived fathers earned their food,
> Toil strung their arms and purified their blood.' "

"Well done, Vicar," George Coventry said. "And amusement which improves the health and gives strength to the muscles of an idle gentleman will do the same for a clergyman."

Havelock's presence in the field had been a welcome sight to squires and yeomen as "Hark-in", "Hark yoi" sounded on the crisp morning air of Beckford and Ayshon. Gone for a while as he sat mounted on the Squire's thoroughbred were the clerical waistcoat and black single-breasted outer garment, giving way to more fitting garb. In the parishes, too, he was popular. A man who would smoke the long pipe, drink deep and long from the pewter tankard at a wayside inn was acceptable at Ayshon and Beckford. Richard Surman smiled the smile of an old man giving way to the young as Moses gave way to Joshua. A touch of envy, perhaps, but it was inevitable.

When the hounds met at Croome Court, the other side of Bredon Hill with only Avon's river to break the great plain between there and the Malvern Range, favoured followers came the night before the meet, hacking from the countryside around to arrive for four o'clock dinner. Havelock, Hedgecock and Lord

Waterford were among the diners. George Priddey, the whipper, hobnobbed with the gentry, and Savoury, his favourite hound, followed at his heels. Songs were sung, the November ale flowed freely, the portraits of horses and dogs, foxes' masks, stags' antlers shone in the light of a great lamp hoisted to its place by a thick rope. There were ancient timepieces, quaint in their way; rare birds in cases; the Coventry ancestors, grim and old, portraits of men in stiff starched frills, large vests, small hats.

William Havelock viewed the scene and realised it was only late afternoon and that the guests of Lord and Lady Coventry were booted and spurred ready for the hunt. He enquired of Priddey why this was.

"Bless the Reverend Gentleman!" Priddey said. "We shall not leave the table all night. We'll eat and drink and sing and tell tales of long ago, and then before the fog has lifted and the rime melted in the sun, we'll be after reynard in yonder cover — Tydlesley Wood, to be exact. 'Twould be a great delight to me to take you at another sport, Master Havelock. Am I right in saying you like hawking on horseback on Bredon Hill? Ah, 'tis fitting for a parson to hunt with a sparrow hawk, a quick flighted bird, to be sure."

Priddey was described by Havelock as "a foxy man — foxy all over."

> His conversation had no other course
> Than that presented to his simple view
> Of what concerned his saddle, groom or horse.
> Beyond this theme he little cared or knew.
> Tell him of beauty and harmonious sounds
> He'd show his mare and talk about his hounds.

A tie-pin he constantly wore was little smaller than a saucer, made of china with the head of a fox on it. His bachelor bedroom was hung with sporting prints, foxes' brushes and other souvenirs of the hunt. His roundish face, scarred by smallpox, had two eyes which twinkled like the stars he often rode beneath. He would rehearse the day's sport in the servants' kitchen with wonderfully modulated Tally-ho's or Who-who-hoop, setting the cups and saucers dancing. His tones were as fine and mellow as a French horn. Priddey was a great favourite at the Plough at Ayshon, on familiar terms with Chalk Farm as the score behind the taproom door was called, but he never liked getting into debt and was relieved to see the sponge wipe out his score.

But Priddey, like his master Lord Coventry, grew old, became weak and was granted his last request as his days as whipper-in ended. Tom Priddey went the way of all flesh on 29th October, 1806. His hunting friends said that "he was as good for rough or smooth as ever entered Ayshon Wood". He died brave and honest as he lived, loved by all, hated by none that ever knew him. His farewell glass was a toast to the success of fox-hunting for ever.

When he was buried at Croome by the Rev. William Havelock, he had been whipper-in to Lord Coventry for twenty years. He was carried to his grave by a proper number of earth stoppers—six in fact—attended by many sporting friends who mourned him. Close behind the corpse followed his favourite horse, Old Soul, carrying his last fox's brush in the front of his bridle, with his cap, whip, spurs and girdle across the saddle. Then came two couples of the oldest hounds in the pack. After the ceremony, as he had wished, he had three rattling "View halloos" over his grave.

Death came again to Croome the following year when Lord Coventry, who had done so much for Severn and Avon Vale and Cotswold Edge, passed peacefully away leaving George as the new Lord of Croome Court. Priddey's love of horses was fully shared by his master. In his will Lord Coventry wrote: "After my burial at dusk in the evening, that is, as soon as convenient after, my chestnut horse known as Rufus shall be shot by two persons, one of whom to fire first and the other to wait in reserve and fire immediately afterwards so that he may be put to death as expeditiously as possible, and I direct that he shall afterwards be buried with his hide on and that a flat stone, without inscription, shall be placed over him."

These wishes were carried out. Lord Coventry's body was carried by estate workers for burial by torchlight in the family vault at Croome church near the ivy-mantled tower. The funeral service was conducted by the Rev. Richard Surman, Lord Coventry's own vicar of Croome, and the Rev. William Havelock.

Havelock had lost two friends of the hunting field, but George, the new Lord Coventry, Lord Waterford, Andrew Hedgecock and many more kept the foxes moving with the pack on Bredon Hill, at Elmley Castle, Broddy Castle and beyond. The covers rang out with the music of the horn, the baying of the hounds from cub hunting in early Autumn until Easter.

Back at Ayshon, Surman's health was causing concern, which meant that Havelock had two churches to preach at most Sundays. This, with christenings, marriages, the churching of women, burials, communion for the sick and taking Richard Surman's place as schoolmaster to the sons of farmers, kept him busy. He couldn't always attend the meet of the fox hounds.

During the hunting season of 1808, on a Saturday when the hounds met at the invitation of the Hedgecocks at Sundial Farm, Adam Bosley and Mary Thomas decided to marry at St Andrew's at Ayshon. William Havelock knew full well that the wind, being where it was, due south, the fox from Ayshon Wood would make by way of Church Close to Beckford Coppice. He arrived early at church in his hunting garb, jack booted on his mare, Polly.

Jack Baker now a very old man but still Parish Clerk, was amazed to see him but soon realised Havelock's intentions. "Take Polly, Jack, and hold her by the vestry door." Havelock then put on his surplice over his hunting pink but his jack boots showed beneath as he stood at the altar rail. Adam and Mary stood before him under the chancel arch. The villagers thronged to see this happy union but Havelock was in somewhat of a hurry to run through the service; Jack Baker knew why. At intervals Jack shouted through the vestry door to the vicar: "They be a coming through Primrose 'Ood. Now I yurs um on Holcomb Nap."

As the pair entered the vestry, the service over, Havelock declined the offer to partake in the wedding breakfast. He declined his fee. He mounted Polly, threw his surplice to Jack and joined the field as the hounds made music to him sweeter than the village orchestra or Jack's pitch pipe. He hunted, as was expected, to Beckford Coppice. There the hound ousted their fox who went over the hill towards the river at Eckington. With all his faults, Havelock was loved at the two villages.

The Death of The Rev. Phil Besford

After a Christmas of failing health and the departure of his housekeeper, Mary Barnes, who had gone to live with a niece in Oxfordshire, Phil Besford died soon after the harvest home of 1805. He had been a favourite in Ayshon parish, farming his holding after finding life in agriculture more to his liking than the life of a parson. It was his wish to be buried at Oxford, the home of his father, the place where as a young man he took his degree. Now George Hedgecock thought it right to send someone from the village to represent him at the funeral. Lord Coventry's son came over from Croome with a message from his father. It was

Lord Coventry's wish, and Lord Waterford's wish as chief land-owners of the district, that Ayshon should be represented at Phil's funeral. George Hedgecock, who had all his corn in rick and abarn, had no hesitation in sending his younger son, Andrew, to Oxford with his grandson, Peter Trusswell.

"Two useful gentlemen," Harry Steel commented to Lijah Hicks in the Plough. "How be um a gwain?" Job Allen asked. "From the h'Angel at Persha?" Job was right. Adam Bosley drove them over in one of Hedgecock's vehicles to meet the stage coach. The Rev. Phil Besford in his coffin had gone by way of Burford.

Andrew and Peter took enough change of clothing, enough money, to last much longer than a mere fifty miles to Oxford.

"Thee waits until they gets thur feet on the Oxford Road," Adam Bosley told Hedgecock's men when he returned to Ayshon.

Somehow George Hedgecock had a feeling that his cuckoo lamb, Andrew, and young Peter would be away longer than it took to bury Phil Besford. Tom Steel had proved himself to be an honest and industrious man, so George put him in charge of the Sundial Farms until Andrew's return. When the Worcester coach left the Angel at Pershore, the usual stages were called upon. There was change of horses, watering of horses, drinking and eating at various inns. Broddy Hill was a challenge for the horses but once on the flat of the Cotswolds the coach moved quickly to Oxford. For men like Andrew and Peter it was suffi-cient to attend Phil's funeral, to pay the respects of the Ayshon folk; the spread afterwards was attended mainly by members of the clergy and a few of his relatives. Andrew and Peter found lodgings for the night at a posting house in the town—the Mitre. Next morning they decided not to return on the Worcester coach but take the Mail Coach which called at Oxford from Milford Haven and Gloucester and then on to London.

"A while in London won't do us any harm," Andrew said. "The Steels, the Hickses, the Bostocks can cope at Sundial Farm."

The journey to London was uneventful, terminating at the White Bear, Piccadilly. "We may as well stop here," Andrew decided. "It's central for us to see the sights and food's good I'm told."

The White Bear was indeed celebrated for its dinners, for coaching men were good trenchermen. Peter took note of the fare, a boiled round of beef, a roast loin of pork with peas pudding and parsnips, a roast goose and a boiled leg of mutton.

"Go easy with the parsnips, Peter," was Andrew's advice as they wallowed through the fare. "They do say that parsnips make a man crave for a nice young woman and this place swarms with butterflies."

"Who's talking?" Peter replied, his mouth oozing gravy. "It's no secret at Ayshon about you ravishing the maids at Sundial; if only Aunt Catherine's husband knew he would preach you a special sermon at church."

The young Ayshon men rose early the following morning when Autumn made itself felt in London as in other parts of Britain. It was customary to walk in the parks at given hours and here Andrew and Peter found excellent company with the ladies; then tea with their partners; then to the theatre. This was life for the yeomen of the west midlands— the life of the cobbled streets, of cabs, of silks and satins, of gin palaces, of nights between lavender-scented sheets, of men in uniform. When the candles had burnt low in the White Bear, Andrew and Peter escorted the daughters of London merchants back to their homes in the fashionable West End and, with another nightcap, so to bed.

"After Regent's Park, the Vauxhall Gardens are a place to be seen," a waiter at the White Bear said, and it was an education for young Trusswell to see how the gentry lived in London. There were thousands listening to the music of the bands, making love, singing and fighting. Then a day at Tyburn to watch the hangings, which were always well attended. As the death cart approached the scaffold, old ladies just deigned to raise their eyes from knitting to see some poor mortal strangled by the hanging noose.

Sunday in Ayshon was for the most part a day when the labourers of the fields rested. The parson dined well with the squire after church service; yeomen like the Hedgecocks dressed in their best, attended church, ate and drank and slept the day away; poachers took beast and bird off Bredon Hill as keepers relaxed their watch on the preserves. But London on Sunday taught Andrew and Peter another lesson. They knew full well that gambling was a weakness of the richest of men but they also found it common amongst the ordinary people. Brutality flourished in daylight, gentleness lived in the shade. Executions and whippings were everyday spectacles, bull-baiting and dog-fighting and dog-hunting were usual during times of Sunday services. The upper classes of the great city found Sunday afternoon entertainment with their families at the old Bethlehem Hospital, watching maniacs chained naked to the pillars. Every Sunday afternoon 200,000 people gathered in London's tea gardens, by nightfall 50,000 could be classified as still sober, 5,000 as dead drunk. In the circles of London life it was unusual for a party to break up while one member was still sober. The streets at night were littered with footpads and prostitutes. How the young gentlemen dealt with the latter, they never said, but Peter did remark one evening that he would go out alone, late, through Piccadilly.

"Bread and bread is no good, Andrew," he said. "Bread and cheese would be better." Andrew warned him of the ways of women and persuaded him to leave most of his golden sovereigns with him.

A young, handsome man like Peter was venturing on dangerous ground when he was set upon by a footpad in the dim London Street at an hour when the Hedgecock household would be thinking of getting from their beds for the morning milking, the feeding of the stock. Lijah had always told him as a boy not to let his mother think she had bred a jibber, never to be afraid of anyone, not if they were as big as a house, and, in the true tradition of noble art, Peter gave the footpad left and right to the chin, then another to heart and left him curled up on the cobbles like a bundle of washing.

"Parsnips for passion," he told Andrew next morning. "I could take on almost anyone barefisted on the food we are having at the White Bear."

"Tonight," said Andrew, "we'll go and see how the prize fighters shape. They are fighting for a belt at one of the halls."

Here Andrew and Peter took notice in detail how the professionals fought toe to toe, round after round until one had to give in. "Some difference in speed and motion to our chaps at Ayshon on Boxing Day in Finches Piece," Peter said, adding, "Still, I suppose it's bloody noses at Ayshon, same as London."

They wondered what was still to see in the City. "The races," Peter ventured. "We might make a few sovereigns there."

A chaise was hired from the White Bear to take them to a meeting just out of town. Here they gambled heavily and were lucky not to lose all their money. Some they recouped at cards that night at their lodgings. Next morning after breakfast, Andrew told the landlord of the White Bear that they would take the Worcester coach on the following morning. That night, London went mad. News had just come through that Lord Nelson, Admiral of the British Fleet against the French and Spanish, had won a great victory at Cape Trafalgar, but had been mortally wounded on his flagship as he stood resplendent in all his colours on the quarterdeck. Never again would Britain be in danger of invasion; the French fleet was scattered and beaten by Nelson's men. The English Channel would now be safe, the British could relax their measures against imminent invasion. Peter and Andrew sat in the White Bear and supped their Madeira, pondering in their minds that evening how many Ayshon men were with Nelson at Trafalgar, some Holmes' boys, some Bradfields, but not young Bosley, he would now be swinging the flail making a start on threshing the Hedgecock harvest.

The Worcester coach left early. Peter and Andrew didn't know Hounslow Heath from Uxbridge, but Hounslow was the first stop for all coaches plying westward from London. Hounslow Camp became a favourite holiday amusement for Londoners and here were kept the finest array of posting and coaching horses to be seen—2,500 in all. It was an awkward place to get away from in a fog. The ostlers told the Ayshon men how the mails from London were escorted out with torches, eight mails following one another, the guard of the foremost lighting the torches one by one until they were all lit; three hours it took, he said, to do nine miles. The Worcester coach broke its pole and went down a steep embankment, the two nearside horses were drowned in a brook and the coach came to rest on the stump of a willow tree. Fortunately no passenger was injured. Refreshed, the horses and passengers drove on into Buckinghamshire. Hard and fast the stage coach fled over hill and dale, racing the Mail as it sped along.

Andrew and Peter decided to spend another night at the Mitre at Oxford with its broad corridors, snug bars, four-poster beds hung with silk, sheets smelling of lavender, choice cookery and claret, all equal to the best that could be obtained in London. Here there was a motley crowd of statesmen, generals, poets, wits, fine ladies, highwaymen, conspirators and coachmen, worthies of the road, dressed in full bottomed coats, beavers, top

Felling an oak: the tree has been barked for tanning.

The Battle of Trafalgar, a contemporary engraving.

boots, periwigs, eating, drinking, flirting, quarrelling, delivering up their purses, gambling over bills. Here was the finest cross-section of the people of Britain.

Next morning the Worcester coach called at other posting houses at Witney, The Bull at Burford, then on for Stow-on-the-Wold. Near here lived a Mr Freeman of London who kept a large house with a staff of servants and entertained lavishly. This popular and hospitable Mr Freeman and three of his retainers were highwaymen who had worked the home counties for years. Now, as the Worcester stage coach left Stow for the Evesham Vale, Freeman and his men stopped it with the usual "Your money or your life" cry. How lucky it was for Andrew and Peter that their money had been spent in London! Freeman and his men took the purses and bags of all on the coach, then rode off with their booty, faces masked, to their big house near Stow.

So penniless, Andrew and Peter left the coach at Pershore's Angel Inn and walked six miles to Sundial Farm. As they viewed the summit of Bredon Hill in the gathering dusk, they saw that the people from the hill villages had just lit a bonfire near the Folly to celebrate Nelson's victory. Phil Besford's funeral had been a long and costly business.

Old Oak

The Rev. William Havelock kept Ayshon and Beckford informed regarding events abroad. He took comfort in Nelson's victory at Trafalgar three years before but was well aware of the war Britain was waging against the French in Spain—the Spanish Ulcer, Boney called it. By the end of 1808 the British forces under Wellington, or Sir Arthur Wellesley as he was then, had no powder left; with cold iron they drove the French forward. Up

till now, said Havelock, our land forces had done little compared
with the great British Navy.

Lord Waterford and William Havelock, chief landowners of
Ayshon, consulted with George Hedgecock about the need for
oak to build more and more ships for the British fleet. The
Ayshon men, impoverished by the war, were loyal to their King
and Country. "If it's oak they want," they said, "we won't
spare any for our own use, the Navy shall have it all." Soon the
sound of axes rang through Ayshon Wood, the ring of the saws
sent the rabbits scurrying to their holes in the coppices. Men
experienced in timber came to Ayshon village. As great oaks
crashed to the ground, the bent branches were prized most of all
to form the timbers of the warships. Bent timber, grown that
way, was more durable than that sawn across the grain. The
dockyards were glad to get the Ayshon oak. Jim Bradfield and Job
Allen, the two oldest men in the village, declared at the Plough,
"Ayshon oak is terrible tough— As hard as hell's bells." Then
they agreed on the truth of the old saying about the weather—
The oak leaf out before the ash, in the Spring we shall only get a
splash. "That's rain in the Summer," Jim said. "Oi, and thee
knows't what happens when 'tis the other road round," Job
Allen said. "The ash before the oak, we shall sure to get a
soak."

"I a noticed that," broke in Harold Holmes, "and I'll tell ya
summat else about oak. I a bin holding the plough tails this forty
odd years and when I speaks a ploughs I myuns the 'ooden ones
with no wheels. Now if you a got oak trees to contend with on
the arable, it uzzy— just plough up to the butt of the tree within
inches and no roots will bother ya. The roots of the oak goes
straight down into the ground. They be anchored. Now with
elm, 'tis different. The roots spread ten yeards away from the
butt and they be shallow at that."

"What a that?" young Adam Bosley spoke up boldlike after several pints of Vale's beer.

Harold marked out an imaginary furrow on Vale's stone slabbed kitchen floor, his stick indicating a straight line from the barrels to the door. He placed a chair where the elm would be, a little away from the straight line, then around the chair he laid shepherds' crooks, walking sticks, broom stays, all representing the roots of the elm. "Now look yer, chaps. The four hoss team ploughs a fresh furrow from the barrels to the door, the sticks be hidden elm roots. The plough share, as it turns over the top six inches of soil, runs under one root after another and what happens?"

The stockmen, the shepherds, the grooms, who had never had the feel of plough tails, were speechless. David Steel, over for the evening from Croome Court where he was Lord Coventry's butler, dressed in foppish clothes, his lily-white hands holding a mug of ale, said that Harold was making a tall story out of a few elm roots, almost as tall as the elms themselves. Only Job Allen and Jim Bradfield knew the meaning of all this but they just winked at each other as they blew the froth off Vale's best beer.

"Ever sin a ploughman with his front teeth knocked out?" Harold asked Vale's customers. "Well, I have, 'cos when the ploughshare slides under a tough elm root with some good hoss flesh in front of the plough, the plough tails rear up in the air and if you don't loose em smartish like they ull make your bottom jaw rattle. I ud like to see thee, David Steel, holt of a long plough with your ladylike hands walking the furrow with your buckled shoes — still, every man to his own trade, dare say I'd make a hag carrying a tray of wine glasses. But never forget your upbringing. Your old father have forgot more about farm stock than we shall ever know."

Regardless of the talk in the Plough, it was the Ayshon oaks that were felled for shipbuilding; the elms were in demand but most stood upright still, upright as soldiers.

George Hedgecock left the felling of the trees on Sundial and Ayshon Wood to his sons Andrew and Mark. The two yeoman farmers had come to an agreement with their landlords that the landlord owned the trunk or butt of the tree, while the tenant had the head. These arrangements varied in different districts but in Ayshon the tenant had the head of the tree to compensate for damage to fences as the trees crashed to the ground, and damage to crops where the fallen head of the tree lay. The tree feller, or the man who wielded the axe and used the saw, had the chips of wood he made with his axe for himself. In the case of oak these were good for the fire or for burning on the hearth if bacon was to be smoked.

Trees doomed to be felled were marked by the men who knew at a glance what was suitable for the shipyards. There was great activity in Ayshon and Beckford as 1808 drew to a close. Harry Steel and Lijah Hicks wept as the row of sturdy oak crashed into the home ground at the bottom of their gardens. "No more shelter and shade for thee and me," Lijah said to Harry. "But who be we to complain at our age, if they wants the ships they must have timber, I suppose."

Surman, preaching at St Andrew's, tried to console his flock about the loss of the oak. "Ayshon," he said, "is mainly a parish of ash trees and with the elm and the young oaks, we'll soon fill in the gaps."

Jim Bradfield, Job Allen, and Jack Baker met George Hedgecock outside the church. "Master Hedgecock," Jim said, "You a bin a farming man all these years, you had a bit a schooling as a bwoy, now can you tell we chaps how long it takes to grow a good oak tree, 'cause I reckons it takes a hell of a long time."

George Hedgecock tapped his walking stick on the bottom

step of the village cross, cleared his throat and thoughtfully looked on the ground. "It depends, Jim, on what the timber's required for. One a hundred years old may do for some jobs but when they grow for three hundred years, then, like you and me, they start to grow downhill. Some in church close was there in good Queen Bess's time. Then, like all crops, it depends on the soil."

Jack Baker alone looked really worried, then he spoke. "Master Hedgecock, you knows where Mark farms at Ayshon Wood agen the Elmley Castle boundary? There's a big oak in his far side hedge and it's marked for felling."

"No doubt, Jack, no doubt if the ship yards want it."

"Ah, but 'tis the Gospel Oak," said Jack Baker.

"Upon my soul," George Hedgecock whispered as he gently sat down on the second step of Ayshon's preaching cross. "Jack, I'm grateful to you for reminding me. I'll see Mark and Richard Surman, too, tomorrow, and that tree shall not be felled."

Richard Surman was a man who laid great store by tradition. He was not a superstitious curate but to fell the Gospel Oak would be sacrilege to him. Had not he and his flock made a yearly perambulation of Ayshon parish on Rogation days, beating the bounds, saying Psalms 103 and 104, asking his people to thank God if it looked like being a plentiful harvest, and he and his churchwardens calling on God's mercy if they feared scarcity. This they did as, willow sticks in hand, they halted under the Gospel Oak where the Gospel was read and prayers said to save the corn from pestilence and disease.

Lord Waterford and William Havelock agreed that it would be tempting the Almighty to fell the Gospel Oak. Havelock referred to Ayshon's problem as he took the duty at Beckford Church. He said how he admired the sincerity and the wisdom of George Hedgecock and his family and he quoted from Herrick's poem:

> Dearest bury me
> Under that Holy-oke or Gospel Tree
> Where, (though thou see'st not) thou may'st think upon
> Me, when thou yearly go's procession.

So despite the customary mark, the Gospel Oak was left standing on the border of Ayshon Parish. It grew oak apples for Oak Apple day on May 28th commemorating King Charles's escape from the Battle of Worcester; it shed its acorns out of their pipe-like cups as food for the pigs; it grew mistletoe; it blew in the gales and the carrion crow nested in its swinging branches. Ayshon folk were attached to the Gospel Oak. Jim Bradfield and Job Allen surmised that there might be some of our ancestors' bones anant the butt of that great tree. I daresay it's three hundred years old now, Joby,'' Jim speculated. "And them bones don't grind and ache of rheumatics like as ourn.''

While at Ayshon, as in other parishes, the great oaks were thinned out of wood and hedgerow for timber for the dockyards, the war on the Continent dragged on. After Wellesley's advance, as his forces helped the Spanish to drive the French back into their own country, the French counterattacked, pinning down the British on the Corunna peninsular. Sir John Moore, who was in command, was killed but the French were forced to retreat while the 15,000 British troops were able to sail for England unmolested. Richard Surman, whose health had improved, kept up with the news from Spain, in fact, Ayshon folk talked of little else. Ayshon men were numbered among the British troops, and Colin Surman, the Reverend's son, George Hedgecock's grandson, was serving as a junior officer on one of the British warships which took off the troops from the peninsular, troops who had fought many battles and marched hundreds of miles. Colin Surman was proud to be serving on a man o' war; proud to be living on English oak.

As the fleet left Corunna, Colin took his station on deck to meet the full force of Biscay's wrath. On that late January day in 1809, with just enough canvas for the following wind to drive the ship over the waves, Colin's thoughts went homeward to Ayshon, to his Uncle Andrew at Sundial Farm, to Uncle Mark Hedgecock at Ayshon Wood, to his old grandad and grandma, now retired. Ah, he thought, as the timbers of the great ship creaked in the swell, I daresay Dick Hicks is ploughing Staights Furlong, or maybe the Dean or Cinder meadow. The furrow our ship makes reminds me of that except that our furrow goes both ways, not just to the right, and then it fills in again astern but we are ploughing the ocean with one long furrow from here to Britain. The creak of the timbers remind him of the noise the trees made in the Close as branch rubbed branch. When men spoke of the crows nest up on the top of the rigging, Colin thought of the carrion crows at home, building their lone nests in some quiet spot; then the huge rookeries, like small towns, in the hedgerow elms. As the fleet moved northwards, Colin remembered his father. Speaking to him of the shipbuilding yards as a boy: the shape, the size of the timber, the soaking of it in vats of brine. Then how what small crevices there were between the planks were filled with tar and oakum. Richard Surman had visited the county jail and seen Ayshon men picking oakum, picking apart odd bits of rope into little pieces for caulking the crevices in the ship's sides. As the ship rolled from side to side Colin remembered Lijah Hicks on the black mare, Blossom, riding home sidesaddle after a day harrowing the wheat—or some of the regulars, with rolling gait, homeward bound from a Saturday cider session at the Plough. When his ship pitched and tossed, wasn't it like the loaded waggons of Hedgecock's hays crossing the ridge and furrow of their West Midland farm? In dry dock. Colin had watched limpets being scraped off the sides of the vessels. "Parasites," he thought, "can't leave the oak alone." Mistletoe fed on the branches of the Church Close oaks, but mistletoe liked the cider apple trees in Grandad's orchard best, then the hawthorn on Bredon Hill. Bredon Hill, where as a boy he found fossils in the parish quarry, fossils of sea creatures thousands of years old when it was said that the Hill was under the sea.

When the troops sighted land they crowded to the port side. The boat listed as if the oak were bending again as the branches bend on the growing tree. What will Grandad Hedgecock want to know when I get to Ayshon? It's hard to describe life at sea to a farmer. I'll tell him, thought Colin, that the felling of the oaks on his farm was not in vain. We (the Navy) have brought back to England 15,000 men, some wounded, and we've all travelled on English oak.

George Hedgecock Remembers

George and Anne Hedgecock felt Colin's return from Corunna should be celebrated, and when he returned to Ayshon the family and all his friends were invited to a party, along with Harry and Esther Steel and Lijah and Jane Hicks. As the gathering would be too great for George Hedgecock's small house, Andrew and Barbara welcomed them all at Sundial Farm. Lord and Lady Coventry came over from Croome Court, bringing David Steel, their butler, with them. Colin had brought back from Spain some of that country's choicest wines, which added something special to the occasion.

After a beautifully prepared evening meal, the food served by Barbara's maids and the wines by Butler Steel, George and Anne Hedgecock seated themselves on one side of the inglenook as sparks from the log fire leapt up the open chimney. Lijah and Harry were invited to sit in the opposite ingle. "We're but two labouring chaps—it yunt fitting for we to sit anant the fire," objected Lijah, but Lord Coventry told them to be seated: "You are important guests tonight."

The wine flowed and the talk went on as merrily. Lady Sarah Fitzwilliam, still hale and hearty at eighty-eight years of age, had joined the party in fine form; the tongues of Lijah, Harry, George and Anne were well loosened. George Hedgecock's mind went back to Cosgrove on the Cotswolds.

"You worked for my old dad, Lijah, didn't you?"

"As a bwoy chap I did, Gaffer, and a good man he was too. Wonderful crops a sainfoin he grew for the Cotswold ship. I can still see the crimson bloom covering the sidelong banks, 'twas a pretty picture."

Harry found that the wine glasses needed more delicate handling than the mugs and tankards at the Plough, but he fumbled happily, emptying one after another, and watched how deftly his son David served first the ladies, then their husbands.

"Lijah," he said, "talking a crimson sainfoin, this yur wine reminds me a that colour, but 'tis the Cotswolds for sainfoin."

"Yes," put in Anne Hedgecock, "I remember the first lot George planted—sowed it with the Spring oats."

"Of course you all know where it originated?" ventured Lord Coventry, who had studied agricultural history more than most. "France; it's called saint foin or Holy Hay over there. But we'd better not talk of the French in front of young Colin."

"The French would be all right if it wasn't for Boney. He's plain greedy, but he will bite off more than he can chew one day. We've captured some of his fleet and we'll have more yet." Turning to Lijah, Colin told him how he had thought of Dick Hicks at plough as their ship ploughed a furrow from Spain.

Anne's thoughts were still dwelling on Cosgrove. "It was a hard life scratching a living on that limestone. And turning the butter churn, then making the butter into moulds for the market, with our special mark on the butter pats."

"Oi, then what became of it, marm? Your humble Lijah took it by packhorse to London."

"Surely not all the way to London?" said George Coventry. "It must be ninety miles."

Lijah took his Madeira in quaffs rather than sips and as he put down his empty glass, hoping that David Steel would soon refill it, he wiped his now toothless mouth and gulped out, "Lechlade".

"What happened at Lechlade?"

"Long before my father's time," George Hedgecock explained to one and all, "Packhorses took a lot of the butter on their pack-saddles to Lechlade-on-Thames. Here it was loaded on boats for the London market. Hedgecock's butter was sold there before I was born."

" 'Twas a perilous journey for a young man like me, travelling through the woods at night with me horse and packsaddle, vixen squeaking, owls hooting, badgers grunting. Still," Lijah added, "we wasn't allus alone. We ganged up with other Cotswold men who took the same track to the Thames."

David Steel passed round the tobacco with a basket of clay pipes, and Colin puffed at his clay looking thoughtfully into the fire.

"Perilous taking butter to Lechlade, Lijah? How would you like 32 lb weight cannon balls dropping on the deck from the French fleet? Sir Thomas Moore stopped one on land from the

French guns—they just had time to bury him before we left Spain.''

George and Anne Hedgecock shook with laughter as they watched Lijah's face. The wrinkles had deepened and the wine and the fire gave it a glow like a February sunset. Then a smile broke out on Lijah's face ending with a toothless grin and a wink to his old gaffer. George broke the silence as he told the company how much he admired Colin's bravery and how grateful he was for the Madeira. Then he asked laughingly, ''What was it you brought back cheap from Lechlade, Lijah?''

''Drink, of a sort, Gaffer. Very cheap off one of the boatmen. 'Twasn't cider, 'twasn't beer—you allus gave me a shilling for it.'

Richard Surman took up the joke. ''Dad, you didn't stoop to smuggling on the Cotswolds?''

''What happened in London just before Christmas? Tell us that, George,'' said Anne, who knew the story very well but wanted everyone to know it that night.

''You tell me, Harry, if I go wrong, but Anne means when we went to Smithfield with the cattle. The London road is different now, but when Anne and I first married and Harry and Lijah were growing men, I decided to take a drove of fat cattle to Smithfield market. We started off along that old cattle track, the Welsh Way, the track taken by the Welsh drovers. I rode my horse, Harry and Lijah went on foot. Twenty fat beasts we had of the Gloucestershire breed. Every night we stopped at an inn on the way while the cattle, tired from walking, grazed nearby. We got to Smithfield and sold them well for the Christmas trade; then I rode back to Cosgrove. I had a young wife to come and look after for Christmas.''

''Oh yes,'' some of the younger people chorused. Anne blushed like a young girl as she remembered George's homecoming after so many nights away.

"What about Harry and Lijah?" asked Mark Hedgecock. "How did they get back?"

"Let Harry tell us that. I've told you enough already."

"Please excuse me," said Harry to the two reverend gentlemen. "But I damn near got myself married. Lijah and me stopped the night at an inn in London—can't remember where—but some tart took a fancy to me. A smart chap I was then, mind. We drunk gin as if we was drinking our Gaffer Hedgecock's cider. Lijah went off to bed, and when I woke next morning, damn my rags if this tart wasn't in bed with me, and me with a thick yud. Her fayther by all accounts was a street trader and they wanted me to go in business with them. But I had the idea that one man 'udn't be enough for her and I didn't want no secondhand furniture, so I bolted through London, knowing that the West End was the end I had come in at. Then, as sure as God's in Gloucestershire, I put my hand in and found my pockets empty. What happened between me and the Cockney tart, I don't recollect. This is the first time this tale a bin told."

"And how did you get back, Harry?" Lady Coventry was laughing so much that tears ran down her face.

"On the bwoat to Lechlade as fetched the butter. The boatmen gave me some fittle."

The party for Colin's homecoming was long remembered in Ayshon. The Cotswold tales delighted the older folk, the ladies played the piano and sang, and for others there were card games. Late that night all joined heartily in the singing of God Save the King; then chaises, gigs and various horse-drawn vehicles took all and sundry home to bed while George and Anne Hedgecock, who were staying the night with Andrew and Barbara, sat on for a while in quiet contentment round the fire at Sundial Farm.